Look for other Western & Adventure novels by
Eric H. Heisner

Along to Presidio

West to Bravo

Seven Fingers a 'Brazos

T. H. Elkman

Mexico Sky

Short Western Tales: Friend of the Devil

Wings of the Pirate

Africa Tusk

Cicada

Conch Republic, Island Stepping with Hemingway

Conch Republic - vol. 2, Errol Flynn's Treasure

Follow book releases and film productions at:
www.leandogproductions.com

FIRE ANGELS

Eric H. Heisner

Illustration by Adeline Emmalei

Visit our website at
www.leandogproductions.com

Illustrations by: Adeline Emmalei

Photo Credit, back cover: Kristin Troy at Middle Fork Lodge

Dustcover jacket design: Dreamscape Cover Designs

Edited by: Story Perfect Editing Services – Tim Haughian

Hardcover ISBN# 978-1-956417-00-5

Printed in the United States of America

Dedication

To the brave flyers who fight the flames.

Special Thanks

Amber Word Heisner, Adeline Emmalei,
Steve Lentz @ Far and Away Adventures
& Kristin Troy at Middle Fork Lodge

Note from Author

I grew up and went to college in northern Illinois. Weekend bonfires and burn-piles were a normal occurrence, and the smoky smell of leaves was a telling tale of the season. Moving west, I found that there is a much more dangerous balance between man and nature where fire is concerned.

In the Midwest, we had all four seasons that included tornados, occasional floods, heat waves and freezing winters. In California, I was to find out that it was so pleasant that there is hardly any weather at all… until you get to *Fire Season*. This is when the sunny months of no rainfall turn the hills and valleys into a golden tinderbox, ready to ignite at the smallest spark, be it heat lightning or a tossed cigarette butt. For days or months, there is a very obvious haze in the air and the distinct smell of smoke.

As forest fire prevention has gone on over the years, wildfires have been mostly put out promptly and effectively. The resulting amount of natural tinder has built up to create an environment of hotter fires and more dangerous burns. That is where we are today; a place where the natural landscapes that we have tried so hard to protect and shelter have inadvertently created a hazardous environment, where the fires burn unnaturally hot and then destroy everything we are trying to save.

Eric H. Heisner

August 17, 2021

Chapter 1

A Sikorsky S-64 helicopter flies through the clear, blue skies. Shaped like an oversized dragonfly in the sky, the chopper flies at a tilted-forward position with a long, umbilical cord-like tow-cable hanging from its hollowed-out midsection. Inside the cockpit, two pilots with aviator sunglasses and headphones, sit behind the flight controls.

The pilot sitting in the left seat wears an old, worn-out cap with a set of fiery angel wings embroidered on the front. During the earlier part of his life, Flynn Russell performed as a stunt-pilot for the motion picture industry and then for traveling airshows. He now flies various aircraft as an aerial firefighter. On the backside of forty, he has spent half his life in the air and has never lost his youthful enthusiasm for flying and vintage aircrafts.

Sitting beside Flynn in the right seat of the chopper, Chip Murphy sports a moustache and a full head of wavy, grey hair. His lean features grow taut, as he turns his head to look out the window at the open skies and the ground below. Flynn angles the flight of the chopper and peers down over his shoulder to the length of tether-line hanging underneath. He shifts the control stick between his knees to one side, and the helicopter gradually drifts sideways before straightening up again. Flynn looks over at his flight companion and then grins widely. "She's still down there…"

Below, hanging from the open midsection of the large Sky-crane helicopter, are several tether-line cables that cut through the wind and remain taut from bearing a heavy load. Attached at the end of the tow-lines, soaring through the air like an oversized marionette, dangles a salvage WWII vintage B-25 Mitchell, with its landing gear in the extended position. The veteran aircraft soars along like a child's kite as it suspends from the belly of the helicopter.

Relaxed and comfortable behind the flight controls, Flynn turns up the music in the cockpit and jams to the beat, as the chopper flies the antique military aircraft through clear blue skies.

~*~

Cruising high above the rural landscape of Northern California, Russell and Murphy observe the landscape below. Acres of farms and wineries cut the terrain into plots of land. The communications radio suddenly crackles to life, and a call from base command breaks their attention from the scenery.

"Sky-crane 4086, do you read me?"

Flynn looks at Chip, lowers his dark sunshades and offers a mischievous grin. The radio crackles again, followed by a determined plea from the base controller. "Murphy… Russell, where are you guys?"

The older pilot tilts his head at Flynn, swipes a finger across his moustache and crinkles his brow discontentedly. His hand goes to his headset, and he pushes on the earphone as he speaks into the microphone positioned below his lip. "Yeah, Control… This is Murphy. Go ahead."

There is a long moment of radio static, until the controller speaks again. "Where in the heck are you guys?"

Fire Angels

Chip gazes over at Flynn accusingly, and shakes his head as the flight controller continues his communication, "That danged chopper left the airbase this morning and was supposed to have arrived at its final destination before noon. They have already taken delivery of the water-drop tank and need to install it now!"

Flynn leans over and peers down the tethered-lines to the wartime bomber suspended below, and speaks into microphone. "Copy that. Slight delay, but we are en route." He exchanges a guilty grimace with Chip, as the other pilot continues to shake his head with disapproval.

The radio crackles and the controller comes on again, "Get it there, now! That whirly-bird was needed yesterday. They got a big lighting strike blaze near the redwoods last night and are all set and ready to install that new water tank. A crew is geared up and prepared to take it out as we speak."

Chip looks out the right side window, then over at Flynn adjusting the controls as the radio crackles again. "Russell, Murphy... What is your e.t.a.?

Flynn turns to his upset copilot and swipes his hand across his throat as a signal for their reply to the controller. Chip covers the palm of his closed fist over the end of his microphone, swings it up over his head and grumbles. "Dammit Flynn! This is the kinda horse-shit insubordination that could cost you this job. And mine too!"

Flynn pushes his headphone mic away and looks pleadingly at his copilot. "We just need another few hours, and we can have this thing nested safely at its new airbase."

Chip continues to sway his head in mild disbelief and looks out the windows at the rolling landscape of vineyards and agricultural fields. "I sure hope whoever you're doing this for is worth the favor."

The radio suddenly crackles to life again with the controller's urgent voice. "Guys, I need you're e.t.a. on this. There are several homes in danger on site, and they want to know why this delivery hasn't happened yet."

Removing his reflective sunshades, Chip glares sternly at Flynn. His gravelly voice is gruff with a no-nonsense tone. "We have to drop this cargo, buddy. I don't care if it's in a crop field or a shopping mall parking lot, but it's got to go."

His mind racing, Flynn searches the landscape for anywhere they might safely put down the winged cargo dangling below. The radio crackles again. "What's up, guys?"

Looking at the seasoned pilot seated beside him, Flynn pleads, "Just a few more hours, and we'll have it delivered safe and in one piece. If we try to put it down anywhere else, other than an airport, the federal agencies will have it forever buried in paperwork."

Lips tightening beneath his bushy moustache, Chip looks outside and down at the vintage warplane hanging directly below them. "I don't really care where we get rid of it, but we need to put it down somewhere right now. I thought this little jaunt wouldn't hurt anyone, but to make this side trip now... We got other priorities, and this is off the table."

Flynn studies the GPS mapping on the control console and points out a small grass airstrip just a few miles away. "There... We can put 'er down there."

Resolute, Chip shakes his head and looks directly below for a location to set down their cargo. "Too far, bud... We can let it go right here and drop it in a field, or I cut the lines free somewhere on our way to deliver this whirlybird."

Looking down at the green fields below, it doesn't take long for Flynn to determine the difficulty of retrieving the old airplane again by land. "You'd just drop it from the sky? Wouldn't someone have a few questions about that?"

Chip shrugs and stares ahead. "We were never here."

"If we don't deliver it to someplace where they can handle it properly, it will be a shame for this thing to just rot away like a hillbilly lawn ornament."

His log book open across his lap, Chip leans forward to the console and begins to enter a new set of flight coordinates. "I'm taking control and flying us to our delivery location.

"Come on, man... We can't just drop it anywhere..." Flynn fidgets in his seat while scanning the landscape below.

Chip looks over at him and retorts, "Why the hell not? It hasn't been doing anything else for the past fifty or so years. A few more won't matter too much." Chip puts on his sunglasses again, plants his feet on the anti-torque pedals and takes over the controls of the helicopter. Slowly, they veer away from their path and fly to the west. Chip glances at Flynn, sighs, and then grunts, "Sorry pal... If you could start those engines, I'd let you fly it down."

The offhand suggestion triggers a crazy idea that percolates in Flynn's mind and shows on his excited features. He swipes off his sunshades to reveal a dangerous glimmer in his eyes. "That's perfect!"

Apprehensive, Chip scrunches his moustache, looks at his friend and then down at the rows of farm fields below. "Alright pard... Just put 'er down right here?"

"No... Go up!"

"What?"

Flynn jabs a pointed finger skyward, pulls back the control stick, and the helicopter starts to gain altitude. Astonished, Chip stares at the pilot next to him and exclaims, "What the hell are you doing!?"

"If we gain as much altitude as we can, I think I can fly 'er into that grassy landing strip over yonder."

"Fly it?"

"Glide it… Whatever."

Chip looks out through the front panels of windscreen and shakes his head incredulously. "Are you completely nuts? That unpaved dirt airstrip is for single engine crop-hoppers, not for World War II museum window-dressing."

Tucking his sunglasses away, Flynn begins to unbuckle his seat harness. "I think they'll understand…"

"That old warbird below us might not even hold together long enough for you to dead stick it down there. You'll never make it!"

Flynn slips out from the left seat position and moves to the access door for the cargo hold area. He pats Chip on the shoulder and comments gleefully, "How will we ever know until we try?"

Chapter 2

The Sky-crane helicopter steadily lifts up, gaining altitude. Suspended from the cable tethers, the B-25 Mitchell bomber hangs beneath. Rising through the clouds, the tie lines almost seem to disappear in the puffs of white sky.

Flynn opens the access hatch to the cargo area and looks down through blue skies to the top of the Doolittle Raider type-aircraft. The tarnished grey outline of the vintage airplane hovers over the rural green countryside far below. Still wearing his headset, Flynn speaks into the mouthpiece under his chin to communicate with Chip at the controls. "Okay, buddy, take us up as high as you can... I'll shimmy down there and slip into the cockpit."

The wind swirls under the whirling rotor blades, and rushes past Flynn as the helicopter steadily lifts up higher. Flynn holds one hand to the microphone and hollers into it, "Keep 'er going! When I'm inside and I give you a thumbs-up, let 'er go, and I'll glide it on home."

Over the intercom, a voice comes from the cockpit. "This is a *bad* idea, pal..."

Flynn takes off his headset and tosses it behind him. He removes his faded cap, gives a kiss to the flaming angel wings, then folds it over and tucks it into the waist of his trousers. After pulling on a pair of leather work gloves, Flynn grabs a firm hold on one of the thick metal strands of tether cable that is attached to the dangling airplane. He turns back to the cockpit and hollers to Chip. "Okay buddy, wish me luck!"

Gripping the tow cable with both hands, Flynn extends a leg out and wraps his foot around the line. Like a fireman descending a brass firehouse pole, he steps out over the abyss and drops from sight out through the open belly of the helicopter.

~*~

The helicopter slowly gains altitude, climbing higher and higher through the clouds. Flynn gingerly slides down the thick steel line of one of the tow cables connecting the warbird to the Sky-crane chopper. The wind ripples against his clothes, and the ground below gradually gets farther away as they continue to lift upward.

Descending down the cable, Flynn eventually reaches the wing of the B25-Mitchell and stands holding the line with one hand, boots firmly planted on the tarnished metal skin. He looks up to the wide-open belly of the helicopter and down again to the aged cockpit of the transported warplane. "No changing your mind now…"

Slowly dropping to his knees, the wind blows against his face, swirling his hair and flapping any loose clothing. Taking a deep, rallying breath, he releases his grip on the tether cable and gingerly crawls along the smooth metal wing. Carefully, he makes his way forward toward the cockpit of the vintage warplane.

~*~

At the controls of the Sikorsky helicopter, Chip peers down at the tethered aircraft below and his partner crawling along the leading edge of the wing. He wipes the nervous sweat from his brow, shakes his head and mutters a prayer. "On the wings of Saint Christopher. Grant me a steady hand and watchful eye… That no one shall be hurt as I pass by…"

Fire Angels

His eyes glance to a toggle switch between the seats that reads *cable release*. As the chopper lifts to greater heights, clouds materialize in wisps and sweep past outside the cockpit.

~*~

Flynn creeps along the forward edge of aircraft's wing, gradually making his way to the curved frame of the fuselage. Transitioning from his precarious position on the wing over to the airplane body, his grip slips on the smooth surface, and he quickly spreads himself flat against the airplane's metal skin. The wind currents continue to blow violently against him, and he stays low and tight to the airframe for a moment. Then, Flynn scoots ahead toward the aircraft's nose and reaches out to the window on the left side of the cockpit. He slides open the glass window on the pilot side and takes a look inside. Clothes flapping in the wind and hair blowing around wildly, Flynn looks up at the helicopter above then down at the ground below through the layers of clouds.

Cautiously, Flynn slides down the curved body at the front of the airplane and scoots closer to the cockpit window. Suddenly, his body swings free of the aircraft, and he grabs hold of the edge of the open window. The airplane lifts a wing on a surge of air current and momentarily seems to be flying on its own, as Flynn's body dangles freely from the window. The wind gusts ripping against him almost tear his grip loose, as he pulls himself up and jams an elbow inside the cockpit to brace his precarious position. With determined effort, he gets the other elbow inside the window frame and slowly shimmies in through the pilot's side window.

From above, Chip watches Flynn's death-defying entry into the suspended aircraft. He wipes away the sweat that moistens his brow, as Flynn finally pulls himself up and into the airplane. Letting out a lungful of air, Chip realizes that he's been holding his breath. He snaps alert and then takes a deep gulp of air before murmuring, "You crazy son-of-a... This wasn't a good idea to begin with, and it keeps getting worse by the minute."

Lifting his gaze skyward, Chip continues to steer the chopper up through the clouds. He grumbles sarcastically, mimicking Flynn's tone of voice, "Uh, yeah boss... It seemed like the thing to do at the time... I'll just climb outside and slip down into the salvaged aircraft that we weren't supposed to be air-lifting in the first place... Oh, and yeah, we just unhooked it..." Chip rolls his eyes, as he continues to mutter in disbelief. "That's right, just letting it drop to the ground, hoping for the best... Genius!"

Pulling back on the flight controls, Chip keeps lifting higher while watching out ahead and sneaking peeks below. He looks to the western horizon and, through the layers of thin clouds, can faintly make out the distant coastal terrain. The radio hisses static, and a voice crackles in the headset. "Guys, where are you? They need that chopper delivered!"

Chip peers down at the overhead view of the dangling aircraft between his feet and sighs, "C'mon Flynn, what's going on?" Suddenly, a hand reaches out from the pilot-side window of the warbird and gives a waving thumbs-up. The helicopter pilot closes his eyes for a second and then looks aside to the cable release toggle-switch.

After another fleeting glimpse at the vintage airplane, attached below, Chip groans and puts a reluctant finger to the shielded switch. He flips back the cover and mutters, "Farewell, ol' pal. Godspeed, carry you on wings of angels..." He flips the toggle switch and his heart sinks with the clunking sound as the cables release from the attachments on the chopper. He looks down and watches, as the old warbird slowly drops away from sight through the wisps of cloud cover   below.

Chapter 3

The Sikorsky helicopter and vintage airplane slowly separate from each other, as the connecting cables drift over the wings and fuselage of the B-25 Mitchell. The chopper banks to the western horizon, and the salvaged aircraft briefly shimmers in the afternoon sunlight before it dips a wing and drops to the earth below. Rather than watching the forthcoming landing, Chip flies the helicopter on to the delivery site.

Inside the cut-adrift airplane, Flynn is strapped into the pilot's seat behind the controls. He grips his hands to the yoke and pulls it back and forth to test the range of motion while keeping both feet planted firmly on the elevator pedals. Letting the aircraft drop through the sky at a steep dive, increasing his speed, he listens as the wind whips through the metal skin and rattles every loose rivet along the body.

Flynn glances outside, and observes the age-pitted propellers idly spinning with the rapidly increasing airspeed. As the clouds rush past the windows, he muscles the controls to no effect. Finally, he starts to feel a little response from the elevator controls and pulls back slightly on the yoke.

~*~

The vintage aircraft glides in a steep trajectory through the afternoon sky with its wheels in the extended position, diving downward as the wind whistles through the fuselage. While props wind-mill from the rushing wind, a loose panel at the top of the wing, tears through the rivets and rips away. Flynn turns to look outside the cockpit and sees the gaping hole left in the skin. The existing lines of cable that control the flaps can be seen on the inside of the wing as the yoke is pulled back more to lessen the dive.

Feet pressed to the elevator pedals, Flynn pulls back, attempting to steer the aircraft toward the dirt landing strip carved out from the vast field of crops. The airstream rips through the rattling metal shell of the airplane and the veteran warbird rapidly approaches terra firma. Flynn mutters aloud, "Come on old girl... You've got quite a few years of age on ya, but you should be able to glide better than this!"

Making mental calculations and quickly assessing the unique conditions of the imminent crash-landing, Flynn puts on a lighthearted grin. "What would Jimmy Doolittle do?" Flynn puts a stub of pencil between his teeth and clenches it like a cigar. Catching his reflection in the window he mutters. "You're looking more like Jimmy Durante, than Doolittle." The aircraft continues to plummet toward the ground and Flynn puts every effort into lessening the angle of descent and gaining control of the steep glide.

~*~

A farm mechanic in dirty coveralls steps outside the dome-shaped airplane hangar to look around and enjoy the late afternoon breeze. Hearing something peculiar in the air, his eyes scan the heavens. He suddenly spots the warbird, with wind-milling propellers, on a muted but rapid descent toward the dirt landing strip. Jaw agape, he drops the oil can in hand and stares, dumbfounded, as the antique airplane careens toward him for a dead-stick landing. Blinking his eyes in disbelief, the mechanic gasps, "What in tarnation?!?"

In a steep glide to the airstrip, Flynn stares ahead at the narrow patch of clearing. The details of the surrounding fields and farm buildings become sharp and clear as the airplane's altitude quickly decreases, and the ground seems to race toward him. Flynn murmurs aloud, "Come on baby...!" and pulls back on the yoke with all his remaining strength. Suddenly, the wing flaps lift and, at the last moment, the plane levels out for a rough, but serviceable, three-point landing. Decayed rubber tires under the wings and nose strut kick up dirt and debris that clatters off the metal underside of the aircraft, until the warbird finally rolls to a stop in front of the awestruck mechanic.

His jaw hanging open wide, nearly to his chest, the man in coveralls stares at the vintage aircraft. He can hardly believe that, right in front of him, the rare airplane just dropped out of the sky to perform a landing with idle props. The mechanic makes an attempt to wipe the unlikely spectacle away from his vision with a shop rag, as he watches the powerless propellers slowly spin while the dust settles along the landing strip.

There is a hint of movement inside the cockpit, and the pilot-side window forcefully slides open. Flynn pokes his head and elbow out of the airplane and briefly looks around. He appears quite satisfied and turns to look at the mechanic. "Excuse me, fella! Do you have a telephone here I could use?" Flynn flashes a relieved grin and the flabbergasted mechanic continues to stare at him, unable to speak. As the rotating propellers finally come to a stop, Flynn puts a hand to his ear, mimicking a telephone call. "I have to get a hold of a Colonel at the Confederate Air Force to come pick up this bird."

Eyes wide and mouth still hanging agape, the mechanic stares at the vintage B-25 Mitchell, as one of the well-worn tires gives out with a *pop*, deflates and slowly settles to the ground. The mechanic sluggishly lifts a shaky hand and hooks his thumb over his shoulder, gesturing to the telephone inside. "You c-ca-can place a call inside…"

Flynn reaches inside the cockpit and comes out again with the curled-up bill of his flight cap with the Fire-Angel emblem on the front. "Thanks, pal! I really do appreciate it!" He shakes out the hat and pushes the front of his hair back before pulling it on. Flynn looks behind at the rutted runway, and then pats the old airplane on the metal panel under the window before he heaves a contented sigh of relief. "Hey fella, nice place ya got here…"

"Uh, thanks…"

Flynn notices that the stunned mechanic seems to have finally got his wits about him, and he calls from the cockpit. "You probably don't get many of these old, wartime bombers coming around too often!"

Making a gulping sound, the old man shakes his head. "No sir… No, we don't."

Chapter 4

A Grumman S-2 Tracker aircraft flies low over the treetops directly toward a column of smoke on the mountain horizon. Seated at the controls, Flynn Russell wears a pair of sunglasses and his old Fire Angel cap with a headset pulled over the top. His focus is on the target ahead while he does his approach. The radio distortion crackles in his ears, but doesn't break his intense concentration. "Flynn, we need that air-drop to cut through the line of fire to the southwest... That will help to protect those smoke jumpers..."

The aircraft engines roar and the whirling propellers trail swirling halos of smoke, as the fire-bombing aircraft dives toward the drop zone. Flynn speaks into the headset microphone without taking his hands from the controls. "Coming in on the target now..." As the twin engine water-bomber flies toward the targeted drop zone, the heated updrafts from the raging fire below makes for a bumpy ride. Fingers of flames lick up from the trees, reaching through the smoky haze to light the sky with a glowing-red hue.

Inside the cockpit, Flynn switches on the windshield wipers to push the obscuring flakes of ash from his sight-line. He looks down at the GPS monitor and carefully times his approach. Murmuring aloud, he holds firm on the controls. "Steady old girl... Almost there..."

Buzzing over the treetops, Flynn adjusts his positioning for the aerial drop. Finally, he releases his load of fire-retardant along the inferno's front line. A red cloud billows from the belly of the low-flying aircraft, blanketing the terrain and smothering the flames below.

As the last bit of retardant mix streams from the tank, Flynn heaves back on the yoke to pull the aircraft skyward. His aircraft rises above the smoky clouds and he sees another fire-bombing aircraft inward-bound over the wildfire drop site. The voice from mission control crackles in his headset, "We have ground-crew confirmation. Drop is right on target. Nice job, Flynn!"

The fire-bombing aviator breaks from his intense concentration to adjust the bill of his cap then the headset microphone under his chin. "Alright, copy-that fellas! Tell 'em to follow the red-sticky road to be home for dinner."

Flynn's airplane banks wide around the smoky area as the other S-2 Tracker pierces through the clouds of flame-tinted smoke to dive at the raging forest fire below. It drops a load of billowing, red fire-retardant and pulls up and away. The controller's voice on the headset responds to the fliers. "Ten-four. Bring it on back to base-camp for a refill, and we'll be sure to get those boys home tonight." The radio crackles with static, and the two fire-bombing airplanes form up, wingtip to wingtip, to fly back toward the provisional air base.

~*~

An early-eighties Jeep turns down a gravel driveway and follows alongside a dirt airstrip to a lineup of several dome-shaped airplane hangars. Beside the runway, positioned at the center of the airport compound, is a two-story brick building with a glassed-in observation deck on the top floor. There is a rag-tag fleet of vintage airplanes, a lot of them looking to be surplus military conversions ranging from World War II to Vietnam, parked around the premises.

The Fire-Angel Aerial Bomber Headquarters is tucked in a forested valley amidst the picturesque mountains of central Idaho. Driving past the office building a bit too fast, the speeding vehicle continues to one of the hangars and skids to a crunching halt before the open doors. The lingering trail of gravel-dust drifts by and settles, as the mud-splattered door of the Jeep swings open with a creak. Beneath the opened door, a pair of cowboy boots appears, stepping out to stand in the unpaved driveway. The engine of the Jeep ticks hot as the figure reaches inside the off-road vehicle to grab a duffle bag, and then swings the door shut.

Silhouetted by the daylight, the man looks in through the wide-open hangar doors at an amphibious model Consolidated PBY Catalina. He adjusts his floppy old cap in a sort of a salute to the parked seaplane, and mutters aloud, "Good to be home, ol' girl."

At the back of the hangar, a person outfitted in greasy mechanic coveralls walks out from behind a rack of parts to notice the recently arrived vehicle through the haze of kicked-up gravel-dust. Tony "Wing Nut" Childs is the all-around handyman and mechanic for the Fire-Angel fleet of water-bombing aircraft. He moves toward the sunlight outside the hanger doors and calls to the man standing in the entryway. "Hey there, Flynn... I heard you were all wrapped up with that freelance gig in Arizona."

"Yep. Just got back last night."

Wing Nut steps out from the shaded interior of the hangar and tilts his head toward the tall, brick office structure alongside the airstrip. "The old man put the word out that you were to come see him as soon as you got in."

"Another job?"

"Uh… Not really."

Flynn gets an odd feeling from the mechanic's adverse tone and asks, "What's up? Is there some kind of problem?"

Wing Nut grimaces and looks across the runway to an idle fuel tanker truck parked alongside the dirt landing strip. *"No jobs* are the problem."

The pilot nods, as he looks around to the surrounding landscape of forested mountain terrain and clear blue skies. "Such a beautiful day like this, and no one needs us to fly…" Flynn tosses his duffle bag just inside the hangar doorway before turning to walk the path to the headquarters building.

The mechanic watches a moment and then calls out, "Flynn, take it easy on the old guy… He just got notice that the fuel company won't fill the tanks on credit any longer." Wing Nut twists a dirty rag around his hand, sighs and slaps it against his thigh. He murmurs, as he walks back inside the hangar. "Easy enough to maintain 'em if they don't fly…"

On Flynn's short walk to the office, the quiet solitude of the air base feels less than idyllic… nearly to the point of abandonment. He glances back at Wing Nut, as the mechanic disappears into the shadows of the hangar. Shuffling his boots along the gravel path, Flynn continues on toward the front entrance of the brick building.

Chapter 5

At the Fire Angels Headquarters, Flynn pushes through the pair of double-hinged, screened doors like he's entering an old-time western saloon. He steps into the air base's bottom floor recreation room and looks around the dimly lit tavern-themed setup, titled "The Dump", which serves as an aviator hangout. A rustic pool table sits in the middle of the room, and a foosball table and shuffleboard setup are located near opposing walls.

At the back wall, a Western film styled bar stretches the length of the room. The wall behind is filled with liquor bottles and old photographs of warplanes and fire-bombers. Puffs of dust come up from the aged, wood-plank flooring, as Flynn's cowboy boot heels scuff across the smoothed surface. He makes his way around the empty tables and chairs toward the stairway which leads to the main office on the upper floor.

~*~

Arriving at the top of the stairs, Flynn turns to look at the layout of cluttered desks and tables stacked with papers, overstuffed binders, local maps and U.S.F.S. geography charts. Seated at a double-wide partner desk near the picture window with a view over the airstrip, an older gentleman with thick tufts of white hair sits working. The man at the desk looks up, scratches his head, and his silver locks glow like landing beacons when the sunlight shines through.

Frederick "Old Man" Thompson is a former tanker pilot and the driving force proprietor of *Fire Angels - Firefighting*. Still in good health physically, his advanced age is beginning to show by the slump of his shoulders and the lack-luster tone of his sun-weathered skin which was once a golden bronze. He smiles at the familiar sound of the cowboy boots coming off the stairs and waves Flynn over as the pilot enters the upper office. "Hey Flynn, come on in and have a seat."

Frederick remains seated, and Flynn eases himself into a cracked and worn-out leather club chair positioned opposite the desktop. He looks at his mentor across the piles of papers, and then looks around the room. "What's doin', Old Man?"

The boss turns to glance out at the empty runway, clears his throat and sighs. "We're about all out of business."

Flynn kicks a booted foot up over one knee and nods to Frederick understandingly. "Things have been tight before. Fire season is just warming up. With a few new contracts, we'll be back in business again."

The white-haired gentleman cants his jaw to the side, attempting to hide his grim emotions, and stares at a single piece of paper on his desk. "If we can't get fuel for the planes, we can't rightfully bid on jobs that come up, and we're done."

Flynn leans forward to gaze at the paper across the desktop and then looks to his longtime friend and employer. He puts his hands on the chair's padded armrests and offers his counsel. "There are other companies that can supply us with fuel."

"Yeah, and we've overextended our credit line with all of them, too. No fuel and no aerial fire-bombing contracts."

In silence, the two men contemplate the situation a moment, until Flynn finally sits back in the creaking leather chair and speaks up. "Well... Do you have a plan or something?"

Fire Angels

"While you were gone, I had to make a hard decision. It's not one that I'm very comfortable with." The Old Man looks up from his desktop and stares across the stacks of paperwork at the pilot.

A feeling of dread rises up from Flynn's stomach, and he swallows it before croaking out the lingering question, "What did you have to do?"

Smoothing his hand across the paper in front of him, Frederick looks across the desk at Flynn and bows his head. "Last month, I was approached with the prospect of selling off a good share of the company along with all of its holdings. It was a generous offer and just enough to keep it afloat."

"How much of the company?"

"Nearly a half interest of it with an option on the land, buildings and air fleet."

Flynn sits back in the leather chair and tries to be sensitive to the Old Man's decision and desperate situation. "Yeah, that's bad. How long will that last us?"

"Hopefully, we'll make it through to the end of the year. Maybe a bit longer, if things pick up..."

Standing up from the chair, Flynn walks to the window and looks out over the fire-fighting air base surrounded by pristine valley and forested mountain ridges. He stares outside, not wanting to turn back to look at the paper on the desk. "Okay... What's the catch?"

"If everything is going well and the way it should be, we continue on as before."

Flynn glances over his shoulder, toward the desktop. "And, if we have another bad year, and things don't go well?"

"They will eventually take over the controlling interest. Their plan would be to sell off the fleet, demo the buildings, and build vacation condos all along this valley."

Staring out the window at the broad expanse of unspoiled landscape, Flynn shakes his head, muttering under his breath, "Aww, shit..."

The desk chair creaks, as Frederick swivels to lean back, kicks out his feet, and folds his thick hands across his lap. "And there is one more thing..."

Breaking his thoughtful contemplation of the scenery, Flynn turns to face his friend with a questioning expression. "Yeah... And what's that?"

The older gentleman takes a moment to form the words in his mind, and then he seems to force what he can of a smile. "They're sending over one of their hot-shot aviation business people and some clerical support staff to temporarily oversee our flight operations and procedures."

"Really? Like a baby-sitter?"

"More like a CEO, I guess. My hands are tied on this. They said I could continue my position as Flight Manager, but I'm no longer at the top of this food chain."

"Who is it, and what's the background on them?"

"They're telling me it's some elite, ex-military big-wig with strong ties in the corporate world."

Shaking his head, Flynn steps away from the window. "Damn! That's all we need around here... What's his name?"

The Old Man pushes his grin a bit wider and replies, "You mean, what's *her* name?"

Chapter 6

Days later, a fire-bombing aircraft sits in front of the hangar, getting refueled by a recently-arrived avgas tanker truck. Contrary to the previous impression of the nearly vacant fire-fighting facility, there is now a flurry of activity. Several cars and trucks are parked in front of the various buildings, and ground-crews are at work prepping for the upcoming season. The buzzing hum of a small airplane engine sounds overhead, and an AT-802F Fire-Boss on amphibious floats flies over the Quonset hut-style hangars to come around for a landing.

As his Jeep drives up the gravel lane, Flynn, appearing casually optimistic about the new activity, scans the air base. He pulls in front of the open hangar doors and sees a shiny new sedan, with California plates, parked in his regular spot. Pulling alongside, he steps out of his vehicle and does a quick primping check of his appearance in the dark-tinted glass of the sedan's passenger window.

The double doors at the main building bang closed. Wing Nut walks over and gives Flynn a surprised greeting. "Hey, Flynn! Funny you picked today to sleep-in!"

Looking to his wristwatch, which reads 9:00 a.m., Flynn shrugs innocently. "Why…? What's going on here, Wing Nut? Is there a blaze somewhere I haven't heard about?"

The mechanic stops to stand beside Flynn in front of the hanger doors and looks inside to the Catalina seaplane.

With a nod, he replies, "The new administration just arrived and is putting all the equipment and crew through the paces."

Flynn watches as the Fire Boss on amphibious floats lands on the pink-tinged airstrip and taxies to the far hangar. "Good to see something in the air." He looks to the Catalina in the hangar and notices that nothing seems to be in the works to ready it for flight. "When is it our turn to take a spin?" Avoiding Flynn's gaze, Wing Nut looks downward. The pilot gets a bad feeling from the mechanic's lack of response and asks him, "What is it, Wing Nut?"

"It's not on the schedule."

"What do you mean, *not on the schedule*?"

Just outside the hangar doors, Wing Nut toes the gravel at his feet awkwardly. "They issued a check-ride schedule this morning for all our airworthy aircraft, drop-converted or not."

His stomach turning, Flynn glances to the large seaplane. "What about the Catalina?" He looks back again to Wing Nut. "She is one of the most versatile birds we have."

"You know, I asked them that exact same thing, and all they said was she's too big, too old and too slow."

With a swelling sense of irritation, Flynn grumbles, "That's just bullshit! What the hell are they talking about?"

"I agree. They're all over there with the Old Man now. If you want to hear it first-hand, I just got an earful."

Quickly realizing that he shouldn't direct his mounting frustration at the mechanic, Flynn calms his temper and gives Wing Nut a pat on the arm. "Thanks, pal… It's not your fault. I'll talk with you soon."

Turning on his heel, Flynn marches over to the main building and kicks open the double set of doors with a bang. The first thing he spots is a young kid in his twenties, standing behind the bar, packing the supply of liquor bottles into boxes. He struts across the recreation room, cowboy boots thumping on the wood-plank floor, roughly shoves a chair aside and snaps at the unsuspecting young office worker. "Hey you!! What the hell ya think you're doin' there, Bubba?"

Shocked, the young office assistant blankly looks up at Flynn. As the angry pilot advances toward him, he quickly replies, "I, uh…, am just packing up these bottles."

"Yes, I see that… Why?"

"Because I was told to."

"By who?"

One of the bottles of alcohol is held mid-air, dangling over the partly filled cardboard box. The confused young assistant stares at Flynn, glances to the stairway leading to the upper office, and then looks back at the unfriendly aviator. "You'll have to speak with the Senior Aviation Consultant who ordered all forms of alcohol removed from the premises."

Flynn looks at the nearly full bottle of rum in the hand of the youngster, as it hovers over the other bottles in the box. He steps up to the bar, leans over and snatches the amber-colored liquor away from the worker's grasp. "Give me that!" Holding the bottle at his side, he barks, "Get away from there, and stop doing what you're doing! Where is he?"

The kid points meekly toward the staircase and utters, "Uh… She's upstairs."

Flynn clenches his jaw, turns and stomps toward the set of stairs leading to the upper office. His boots pound on each wooden tread, as he makes his way upstairs.

Chapter 7

At the top of the stairway, Flynn turns the corner into the upper office and stares at the bee-hive of activity in the room. Stacks of paperwork are neatly piled, with unfamiliar office-assistants organizing and filing each piece of documentation. He stands, bottle of rum in hand, looking at the room, as everyone turns to stare inquisitively at him.

Turning from the window that overlooks the runway, the silver-haired owner hesitantly waves the pilot to his desk. A woman, dressed in a skirt-suit, standing next to the boss also turns, but her features are obscured by the bright morning sunlight coming in from the windows behind her. She holds a pen and clipboard poised and at the ready.

Flynn makes his way across the room while glancing aside at the young office assistants going through mountains of paperwork as they organize years of old files. Disgruntled, he grumbles, "How are we supposed to find anything around here, if they pack it all away in boxes?"

Frederick nods his head cordially to his good friend. "Good morning, Flynn. How are you?"

The businesswoman remains positioned with the sunlight shining brightly behind her and looks down at the bottle of rum in Flynn's clenched fist. Frederick moves to his big desk, which is the only place that is still a cluttered mess, and leans down to rest his open palms on the piled surface.

"Mister Flynn Russell... I guess this will be your informal introduction to our new associate, Miss Camille Vanderhaus."

The professionally-attired woman steps away from the observation window and approaches the corner of the desk. Her uptight business suit is in sharp contrast to the easy-going, casual-flyer appearance of Flynn and the Old Man. Camille straightens her skirt and takes a moment to fully look Flynn over, before she emits a cordial greeting. "Hello there, Mister Russell. I see you found yourself a bottle to comfort yourself with during the transition."

Flynn looks down at the bottle in hand and lifts it over the paper-filled desk. He puts it on the corner with a heavy thump and scrutinizes the executive female from head to toe. He nods over his shoulder toward the stairs and responds, "One of your teenaged office helpers was stowing some of our things away downstairs. I took this off his hands."

A hint of a smile cracks across the Old Man's features, as he watches his pilot confront the uptight executive. Unfazed, Camille responds tersely to Flynn's snide remark. "A necessary task, if only for a short time. Things around here will be a little different, until we can find a way to make this seat-of-the-pants operation profitable... If that's possible."

"And how will hiding all the booze accomplish that?"

"Efficiency and dependability."

Confused, Flynn stares at her. "How's that?"

She lifts an official-looking company letter from the corner of the desk and reads it in answer to the agitated flyer. "Each and every employee will need to do a safety-check ride and skills recertification with a company representative before resuming the official duties prescribed to their position."

His temper flaring up again, Flynn looks over at his superior, who stands a bit straighter, but shrugs unhelpfully. The pilot turns back to face the business-woman and grunts,

"Most of the pilots and crew around here were flying before you could even walk."

She grimaces and places a hand high on her hips. "That's fine, but not really a great testament for their age or qualifications." She glances at the clipboard in her other hand. "If they want to keep flying for this operation, they need to check-out through the proper channels and prove their mettle. The best way for that to happen is to remove the distractions."

"What about the airplanes?"

Holding her ground, she recites more legal-speak from the company's mission statement. "Each aircraft will be inspected and evaluated on its merits and value to the operation at hand."

"Don't give me that lawyer crap! We need each and every airplane that can get off the ground."

"We will consider them all according to their merit."

Flynn looks across the desk to the Old Man and asks, "Does that include the Catalina?" Frederick looks down at his shoes momentarily, unable to meet his friend's intent gaze. Flynn turns and focuses on Camille before asking again, "What about the Catalina?"

She leans a hip to the edge of the desk and responds, "The Catalina PBY is currently being assessed for market value by several museum exhibits and warbird collections."

Flynn clenches his jaw, trying not to explode in anger. "Airplane collectors!?!" He heaves several deep breaths of air in an attempt to calm his flaring temper and finally utters, "She is one of our most versatile and valuable fire-bombers. Taking that airplane out of our stable will greatly compromise the size and frequency of payloads we are able to deliver."

Camille remains calm and almost seems to enjoy prodding the agitated aviator. She looks down at her clipboard, reads a bit, flips the page and looks up at Flynn.

"The estimated value of that particular antique aircraft may be determined greater as a wartime collectable than what it has been used for in the past few decades. The implicit cost of maintenance and replacement parts is a huge consideration."

Unable to contain himself any longer, Flynn shakes his head and growls, "This is complete horse-shit!"

Very cool despite the tense confrontation with the pilot, Camille responds, "The value of each and every aircraft will be assessed accordingly. Be sure to attend the scheduled meeting today, and I will explain it to you all at the same time. Your questions will be answered then."

"Yeah? I doubt it."

"For you, Mister Russell, I will try to talk slowly."

The woman's condescending tone causes Flynn's face to flush. He looks to Frederick, who is silently observing. Incredulous, Flynn pleads with him. "Tell me this is some kind of a joke! Are you going to put up with this crap?!?"

The older man runs his thick fingers through his hair and mutters, "Things are going to change some around here. It's probably for the best if we can adjust with them."

Her hand still rested on her hip, Camille stands firm. She turns her stare to the office assistants in the background, and they quickly go back to work at organizing the clutter. Flynn looks down at his usual seat in the worn leather chair across from the desk, and sees a slim briefcase with a small-sized flight jacket draped over it. He looks at her and mutters, "I don't think I like the way things are going."

With a smirk, she shrewdly replies, "Mister Russell, I can't begin to imagine what you were expecting, but we are not a company who will foot the bill for some over-confident stunt-pilot who wants to risk lives and resources hot-dogging around in salvaged warplanes."

Fire Angels

Flynn blushes with embarrassment for a brief moment. "Are you referring to the Catalina?"

"No, I am not."

Her steady glare makes Flynn feel about an inch tall. He cools his heels and swallows hard before responding. "How did you find out about that?"

She shakes her head reprimanding and coldly replies, "Everyone knows about that."

Flynn looks over at his friend, who lowers his gaze and bows his head in reluctant agreement. Recognizing they are referring to the B-25 Mitchell incident, he shrugs meekly and complains to them. "Once upon a time, we could just fly to an emergency hotspot, sign up our fleet of airplanes and get all the water-bombing work we needed."

Clearing her throat with a trifling cough, Camille shakes her head. "Those days are long over, Mister Russell. It's all in the competitive bid for the larger contracts now."

Flynn looks at the Old Man and then back at Camille. "Well, I liked it the way it was."

Unamused, she gives a roll of her eyes. "That's too bad. Things change, and, if you keep this behavior up, you won't have a job at all."

Conceding that the battle is temporarily lost and that his introduction to the new operations supervisor didn't go as well as it could have, Flynn turns away and starts to leave. Camille calls after him with a quiet authority. "I expect to see you in attendance at the meeting today, Mister Russell."

Paused, he turns back to look at her and then nods his consent. Swiping the rescued bottle of rum from the desktop, he grumbles as he leaves. "I'll be sure to put this in a safe spot, so it doesn't get filed away somewhere." Frederick can't help but smile, but, with a stern look from Camille, it quickly fades.

While Flynn marches off, they look around the office space as the assortment of clutter is stacked, sorted and filed. They can hear the pilot's boot heels thundering down the treads of the wooden stairs and then stomping through the room below. The double, screened entry doors bang open and then quietly close with a creak.

Chapter 8

At the back corner of one of the Fire Angels hangars, behind the parked PBY Catalina, Flynn sits with Chip and several other fire-fighter pilots. Seated across from them in a webbed, folding lawn chair is veteran aviator Garrison "Woody" Pyle. He scratches the top of his head, letting loose wispy tufts of hair from his Chicago Cubs ball cap. "She's a real ball-buster."

Flynn finishes off a can of beer and opens another. "That's to put it somewhat mildly. That woman is ready to scrap everything here that can't be sold off for profit or put on display in a damned museum."

Sitting next to Woody, another flyer, Kansas Sam, wearing dark-shaded sunglasses, pipes in on the conversation. "What's the market for adrenaline-junky fire-fighter pilots?"

A heavy-set pilot, Chuck Strode, sits in a folding chair which looks like it will break any second from the hefty strain. He spits in the open trash receptacle beside him and grunts, "Thems just go in the junk pile."

Sam retorts, "Or just get fired."

The group nods in unison, while they gaze out the open hangar doors to the airfield beyond. Floyd "The Fish" Fisher kicks back his chair, stands and goes to the makeshift bar in the corner to refill his empty glass. "Damn, this is bad luck... Ya know, this is the only job I never hated."

Kansas Sam has a sip from his drink and mutters under his breath. "That's 'cause you hardly work at it."

Smiling, Floyd turns around with a freshly-made beverage in his hand. "I work at it twenty-four-seven." With the amphibious Catalina's wide wingspan and its sleek nose looming over the group, he lifts his glass to salute the plane. "Twenty four hours a week, seven months a year."

There is a communal chuckle from the group of pilots, as if they've heard the joking comment from the crazy-eyed aviator more than once before. Removing his Cubs ball cap and smoothing back his thinning strands of hair, Woody pulls it back on and tries to tame the wisps winging out on the side. "I've been doing this flying stuff for so long, I don't think there is any other job I could do, or would want to do."

Kansas Sam adds, "You're sure not an ace mechanic." Woody frowns toward the laughing flier and snorts in reply. "I can do more on these old planes than you ever could."

Reclined back on the chaise lounge chair, Sam smirks. "Sure, sure, Woody. I get paid to fly 'em, not fix 'em."

Chuck's chair creaks under his weight, as he shifts in his seat and adds, "Okay, Top-Gun. You may not get paid to do either, after we hear what this big-wig corporation has in store for us."

Kansas Sam adjusts his sunshades. "What time do we hear about the chopping block?"

Looking at his old-style wristwatch, Woody responds, "Four o'clock." He gives his timepiece a tap and holds it to his ear, listening to hear if it is still ticking.

Kansas shakes his head and looks to the big clock face on the hangar wall. "Why do you even wear that old thing?"

"It was my grandfather's... And 'cause it works."

Sam grimaces. "Mostly."

Fire Angels

Rising from his over-loaded chair, Chuck stretches his back and goes over to the bar setup. He screws the lid on one of the liquor bottles and slips it down into the cardboard box next to a drink cooler. "Well, boys, the saloon is now closed. We don't want them to get the wrong idea, and think we're a bunch of drunken assholes."

Fish laughs as he raises his cup. "Who's drunk?"

Woody adds in, "They don't know we're assholes yet?"

As if everyone is thinking the same thought, they all turn to look at Flynn, and then Chip, who has been unusually quiet. Chip frowns at Flynn and responds. "Don't they?"

Flynn looks around at them and puts on an innocent smile. He tosses his empty beer can in a high, arcing shot across the circle of chairs into the trash bin. "I highly doubt they care anything about what we have to say with regard to the situation, but we'll see."

A long shadow sweeps in from the open hangar doors and stops near the entryway. The coverall-wearing mechanic calls to the men gathered in the back corner of the building. "Hey, fellas... Time to put on your game face. They're saying to get everyone together for the big meeting."

Flynn confirms with a wave and gets up from his chair. "Thanks, Wing Nut. We'll all be right over."

Woody pushes up from his lawn chair and grunts, "Well... I guess, this is it. The end of an era..."

Scratching under his whiskered jowls, Chuck shakes his head and grumbles. "I guess this beats being fired on the telephone or by registered mail."

Finishing off his beverage, Fish walks over and sets his empty glass on the improvised bar top with a hollow thump. "Hell, I've been fired on my answering machine before."

Kansas Sam laughs. "Really?"

"Yeah, and I forgot to check the damn thing, so I didn't actually find out until two days later."

Bewildered, Sam looks at the Fish, then around at everyone else as they start to get up and leave. "Two days? Did you still show up for work?"

The Fish flashes his goofy grin, as he follows them out. "Yeah, I was there. More or less…"

The group of fire-fighter pilots ambles out the hangar doors and walks the gravel path to the main office. Despite the camaraderie of their social gathering, there is a somber mood as they line up at the doorway… two by two, like pallbearers at a funeral.

Chapter 9

The screen doors of the recreation room creak open and the fire-fighting pilots make their way into the main building. Lined up alongside the stairway at the west wall of the room, the young office assistants are standing at full attention. Further back, against the rear wall, Frederick yearns for a stiff drink as he leans on the back bar against the empty shelves. He watches his crew of pilots filter in and greets them with a sarcastic welcome. "Nice of you fellas to finally show up..." He glances at his watch. "Have a seat, and we'll get started."

The group of flyers spread out across the room to take up seats at the few tables with available chairs. Wing Nut sits with some of the other mechanics, and Floyd Fisher skips the nearest chair and plops himself on the edge of the pool table. After everyone is finally settled, Camille Vanderhaus steps forward and purposely clears her throat to address the men. "Hello everyone. Ladies and..." She looks around and quickly realizes that, with the exception of some of her assistants, she is the only female. "Or, should I just say *gentlemen*?" The creak of chairs, amused snickers, and snorting grunts of disapproval travel through the room, as she continues to address the men. "I am not here to break up your macho, *Peter Pan Flying Club*. No, I'm not..." Her gaze travels around the room. "The reason I am here is to attempt to make this business profitable." Her attention lingers on Sam, who still wears his dark sunglasses. "And why are you here, Mister Cool-cat?"

Kansas Sam cracks a lopsided grin and glances around the room. "Honey, it sure ain't for the money."

There is a laugh from the crowd, and Camille waits for it to settle before continuing. "Well, I'm here for the money, and I'm sure as hell going to make it, one way or another. Gentlemen, I won't talk long, as I see you have some prior leisure activities to get back to." Her scrutiny turns to Fisher, who has billiard balls in hand, juggling them over his lap. Camille sneers acutely, as she focuses her attention on Fish. "Gentlemen... When you're all through *playing with your balls*, I will continue."

The outbreak of laughter breaks his concentration and Fisher fumbles the trio of pool balls. They clank together mid-air, then thump on the wood plank floor and roll to the side. He catches the eight ball, places it back on the billiard table, and shrugs a grin. He sits up straighter and politely responds. "I'm listening, Ma'am."

"Cut the cutie-tooty *Ma'am* bullshit! You can all just call me *Sir* from here on out..."

Fisher's wild eyes grow wider for a moment, and he jumps to his feet with a salute. "Yes, Sir!"

With an okay nod, Camille observes the room and sees that she has everyone's full attention. "Let's get a few things straight, right from the get-go." She strides along, in front of the room, and everyone can't help but take notice of the shapely legs extending below her knee-length business skirt. Turning to address the room, she slaps her hand on the bar top with a solid crack. Frederick stands straighter and eases a step forward from the empty shelves, as she barks her first order of business. "This saloon is closed until further notice!"

Fire Angels

There is a general groan that comes from the group, until she locks eyes with everyone in the room, one by one. "Enjoy the weekend, fellas... First thing Monday morning, I want bright eyes, clear heads and some mostly fresh breath. My crew and I will be putting you and all operational aircraft through the paces. I want you to be at one hundred percent, so I can evaluate where to trim the fat and determine who earns a pay stub. To be clear, I am *not* here to make friends. I *am* here to make this a tip-top operation." She glances at the gentleman behind the bar. "And no offense intended to what you've built here, but this will no longer be a *seat-of-your-pants* operation."

All eyes upon him, Frederick puts on a sympathetic grin and smooths his hands down the backside of his trousers. "Golly, I ain't been chewed-on so much since I was married." The comment gets a snicker from the pilots in the room, and someone yells out, "Which time, Old Man?"

Camille pauses to regain everyone's attention and continues. "You may have already heard or noticed that I have a military background and that I am a *real ball-buster!*" As she strides, she pulls back her shoulders, stands straighter, and perks her chest out. "That's a *fact,* you have heard correct. You get just one chance to prove to me that you belong here, or I scrap and replace you."

At the back of the room, Flynn raises his hand, and Camille nods toward him. "Do you have a question, sir?"

"Is this supposed to be a pep talk?"

"Watch it, fly-boy... I hear you're a pretty good pilot." She locks her eyes on him and continues. "Mister Russell... Let me make it *very* clear. If you're not a good soldier too, you'll be put on permanent leave." She raises the volume of her voice, so everyone in the room is sure to hear her clearly. "Believe me... I've heard all sorts of legend-making stories of what you guys can do. *But*, from now on, we fly it by the book, with no alterations or exceptions..." Her gaze travels toward Chip and then reverts back to Flynn. "Gentlemen, that means **absolutely no favors or deviation from the flight plan!**"

Chip swipes his forefinger under his moustache and curls up the end with an understanding smile. "Yes, sir."

"Good. Glad we understand one another." She nods to Chip, and then her scrutiny travels around the room again. "Now that we are clear, are there any questions?"

At another table, Chuck slowly raises a hand in the air. She points to him and he responds, "I hear you're planning to sell off some of our air fleet. How do we fly and do our jobs, if we don't have enough aircraft to do it?"

In military fashion, Camille struts along the front of the bar as she assesses the assembly of pilots and ground-crew. With shoulders pulled back, she turns to address the room. "The reality of the situation is this..." The group is silent, hanging on her next words. "Some of these surplus-military aircraft have appreciated greatly in value as collector pieces. They are now valued more to 'Warbird' operations than they are fiscally worth to us as water-bombing contractors."

Chuck smoothes his hand across his mouth and utters. "Are we planning to get any fresh aircraft brought in?"

Over her shoulder, Frederick stands and waits for any enlightening news that might have been kept from him. Camille glances at the old man momentarily before continuing. "Yes, we are planning to sell off some of the older, medium-sized aircraft and then bring in several more heavy bombers. If we can't go big, we won't get invited to the party and may just as well go home."

Raising his hand up, Flynn speaks out without her officially acknowledging him. "What about the Catalina?"

"There are a few interested parties."

Fire Angels

Anger rises up and tinges Flynn's voice as he replies, "And you'll replace her with what?"

Facing the room, Camille responds. "We have a line on a C-130 that was used by the Forestry Department."

A grumble travels through the room, until Chip adds. "Our runway won't handle something that big."

Camille keeps her stern countenance and addresses the mustached flyer directly. "Yes, those operations will be held out of the air base at Pocatello or a temporary location nearer to the contracted fire defense site."

Chip kicks up a foot to cross over his knee and replies. "So, you plan on splitting up our pilots and ground-crew in different locations?"

Camille nods and recognizes this as one of the first hurdles of dealing with this close-knit group of fire-fighters. "Yes, there will be a rotating splinter group that will primarily be based out of the larger airfield."

Several of the pilots look around at each other and then up to their leader, as he stands with both his hands placed on the bar. He raises an open palm as a signal for quiet in the room, then runs it through his white hair, nods and remarks, "For now, that's the way it has to be. The valley floor can't handle the larger aircraft, and we need those to compete for contracts."

Camille listens and then nods her head to the Old Man. She looks around the room, studying the attentive group. "Are there any other questions?" The room is mostly silent, and she waits a tense moment more before continuing. "Good, then you are dismissed. Have a nice weekend, and be ready to be put through the paces come Monday morning." The hard-nosed business woman offers an off-hand salute and walks over to speak with her office staff.

41

A bit put-off by the new state of affairs, the pilots and crew members get to their feet and make their way outside. At the double screen doors, Kansas Sam stops and looks back at the looted, empty, back bar. Shaking his head at his colleagues as they file through the entryway, he murmurs, "That was about the least fun I've ever had in there..."

As he passes by, Flynn slaps him hard on the shoulder. "Don't worry... There'll be plenty more bad times to come."

Kansas tilts his chin down and pushes up his dark sunshades. "Yeah... It looks like the good times are over, and we better start looking through the classifieds for another job." In a somber mood, the Fire Angel personnel all drift to different parts of the air base.

Chapter 10

A moderately-sized log cabin home sits at the edge of the tree-line, looking out over its own secluded mountain valley. Parked in front of the old cabin is Flynn's mud-spattered Jeep. An old, dusty Cadillac sedan, with its engine still ticking hot, is parked in front of the hitching post. Everything is peacefully quiet, except the rasp of wooden rails from a rocking chair on the front porch.

The crunching sound of feet on dry leaves comes from a wooded trail not far from the cabin, and Flynn steps out in a sweat-shirt, shorts, and a pair of hiking shoes. As he walks over, he eyes the parked car in front of his home and wipes his hair back from his forehead. Looking up to the cabin's porch, Flynn calls, "Hey there, Old Man."

From the shadowed porch, a rocking chair creaks forward on the deck boards, and Frederick Thompson leans out to let the afternoon sun shimmer on his head of silver hair. "Hey, pal... You on the run from any bear this time?"

Flynn smiles, as he climbs the stairs and steps into the shade. He touches a can of bear-spray, strapped around his waist. "Not today, but I have to keep in good shape for the day it happens again." He smiles jokingly at his good friend. "Hopefully you'll be there the next time, and I'll only have to outrun you."

Frederick chuckles and sits back again to relax in the wooden rocker. "After the damn time I've been having lately, it doesn't sound like too bad of a way to go."

Flynn pulls over another rocking chair and takes a seat. "Aww, you've been through worse."

"Yeah, but when you get old and stuck in your ways, like I have, it's not as easy to take." He raises an eyebrow at Flynn and snorts, "We had some good decades, didn't we?"

"Yeah, and a corporate skirt won't be the end of us."

"Well, maybe not for you..." The longtime friends sit in silence, rocking gently in the chairs and staring out at the surrounding trees and mountains. After a while, the older man sighs, "When I first considered signing the contract on this deal, I knew it wasn't going to be pretty." He snorts as he rubs his hand over his beard stubble. "Ya know... I thought things would carry on a few years more like they were, until I corked off in my sleep or something."

Flynn glances over and smirks. "You *are* pretty old... Could happen anytime."

"Thanks." Frederick scratches his neck and murmurs, "It seems they already got museums and airplane collectors coming in left and right to put interested claims on every set of wings and pile of spare parts we got."

"They didn't waste any time."

"I can't blame them, I guess."

"Any takers yet?"

"No. The corporate bean-counters are still weighing the balance sheets for what surplus aircraft they can get on the cheap and convert for us to use as air-tankers.

"Damn accountants want to run everything."

Frederick nods and huffs a breath. "I guess if I had a good accountant, we wouldn't be in the mess we are..."

Fire Angels

Flynn looks out to the last of the sunshine over the mountaintop, as it drops into the tree-line on the horizon. "Well, nothing happens right away. We're just coming into the season, and we still have a few old contracts to uphold. They can't sell off everything, if they still want us to work."

The chair rocks back and forth on the porch a few times, and the old man nods solemnly. "Just sad to see the damned vultures poking through my hangars for antiques. They do have two big birds scheduled to fly into Pocatello next week at the BLM airbase."

"Pocatello isn't too far."

Leaning back into the shadows, the older man sighs. "Yeah... I'm just gonna really miss looking out that bay of red-dusted windows at the comings and goings of you fellas.

Flynn rocks in his chair, reminiscing, as Frederick continues. "It was downright sociable in those olden days. You hear about a burn, you load up and fly to where it was and they signed you up and were happy for the help."

Feeling the weight of his years, Frederick Thompson rocks forward, looks at his younger friend and smiles feebly. "You sometimes didn't have time to shower or change your clothes the whole time... It was old-fashioned, seat-of-your-pants flying in those days. Then, you went home with a wad of cash in your pocket and slept for a week."

"Good times, huh?"

"Remembering them now, they were the best."

Flynn pushes back in his chair, stares out to the faraway trees and mutters, "Kinda hard on wives, I bet..."

"Which part?"

"Any of those things would do it... Or all of them, maybe. Could be the reason she divorced you..."

Frederick's eyes light up a bit, and he smiles happily. "Which wife you referring to?"

Sharing a light-hearted laugh, the old friends rock back in their chairs, creaking them loudly on the wood porch deck. The sunlight fades behind the mountains, and the dusky light of evening brings alive the chatter of the nighttime insects. Frederick looks at Flynn and taps his palm a few times on the arm of the chair. "It was quite the aviation hub for a time. Hell, we'll all be out of a job when they get remote drones to do the bulk of our work."

Flynn rocks forward, reaches out and gives the old man's hand a comforting pat with his own. "You got any plans tonight?"

"Nope." Frederick grins and pushes off from his chair. "Was hoping to have a few drinks too many and then crash on your couch."

Flynn stands and stretches his legs. "Well, come on in. Give me your keys, and you're welcome to it."

They move down the porch and step into the cabin. Inside, lights are clicked on, and the sound of a liquor bottle cap spinning off precedes the rattling sound of ice cubes and drinks being filled. There is a toasting clink of glasses, and Frederick chimes, "To the olden days and good times…"

Flynn replies, "And, to old friends."

Chapter 11

Monday morning, and the Fire Angels headquarters is a hub of activity. Vehicles drive onto the air base and park near the hangars amidst the welcoming sound of multiple airplane engines warming up. At the end of the runway, a water truck sits filling the drop tank of a Grumman S-2 Tracker.

Flynn drives his Jeep up the lane and pulls into his usual spot in front of the hangar. His gaze instantly travels to the PBY Catalina parked inside the domed metal building. Alone and neglected, there is a certain melancholy to the sight of the amphibious seaplane being left out of the activity.

The door of Flynn's vehicle opens, and he swings a booted foot out to the gravel drive. Breathing in the exhaust-tinged air, a sense of serenity comes over the flyer. He pulls a duffle bag from the passenger-side seat and makes his way inside the hangar to change into his flight gear.

~*~

Passing under the wing of the Catalina fire-bomber, Flynn Russell looks up at the large seaplane and touches his fingertips lovingly along the rows of rivets on the metal body. He wears a tan flight suit and a pair of lace up work boots instead of his usual attire of scuffed cowboy boots and jeans. After fondly caressing the seasoned warbird, he exits the hangar and walks toward the office headquarters. In the distance, several airplanes take off from the short runway.

Eric H. Heisner

With a smile, Garrison "Woody" Pyle steps out of the main building and greets Flynn. "Hey, pal, it looks like they already put up the schedule." Woody stops as the double screen doors slam shut behind him, and he shakes his head. "They have us all doing a check-ride with Madame Ball-Buster's official corporate flunkies." Still listening, Flynn looks past Woody and through the screen doors to the room inside. "She brought in some elite 'flight efficiency' suits to help her." Woody points to the bulletin board on the wall by the entry. "Not sure what those specialists expect to find, but ya'd better fly it by the book and keep the bullshit bagged."

Looking over the schedule on the board, Flynn sees a list of pilot names with assignment of times and aircraft type. There is a second list titled: *Water-drop Targeting Proficiency*. After finding his name on both tallies, he looks over to Woody. "I got ya buddy. I'll just do it all by the numbers and not give her anything to latch onto. Those corporate finance people always want to know why so much fuel was burned or why the flight log shows more hours than their predictions."

The pilot chuckles in agreement and gives Flynn a friendly pat on the arm. As he walks to the hangars, he calls over his shoulder. "Good luck! Remember, no fancy stuff…"

Flynn looks affectionately toward the airfield and muses to himself. "Yeah, pal… No matter how much I think they might deserve it, no funny stuff."

~*~

Over the course of the week, different types of water-bombing aircraft come and go from the dirt-graded airstrip which is stained to a pink hue from residual fire-retardant. Fire-fighting aircraft taxi to and from the runway, as a fuel supply tanker and water truck standby to refuel and refill them. Most of the well-used, former military airplanes are 1940's and 1950's vintage. The whole valley is abuzz, as radial

Fire Angels

piston engines roar through the sky, thundering over the treetops to make their drops on practice targets further afield.

~*~

A week later, a semi-trailer truck with a crane-arm attached to a flatbed slowly rolls up the gravel drive to the Fire Angels Headquarters. Stopping in front of the main building, the air-breaks let off pressure and send a puff of gravel dust into the air. As the truck sits idling, the sight of the flatbed and hoisting gear attract attention from nearly everyone on the base.

Inside one of the hangars, Flynn and Kansas Sam lounge in folding lawn chairs and watch from across the way, as the driver of the big rig climbs out with a bundle of paperwork. Clipboard in hand, the driver enters the office. Studying the lift-crane on the flatbed, Flynn shakes his head. "Now, what the hell is that?"

Sam sighs heavily and responds in a somber tone, "Looks like they're scrapping out a lot of parts or one of our fire-angel wings didn't make the cut."

Rising up from his chair, Flynn stomps his foot and curses. "Gol-dammit! This is bullshit!" He marches over to the main office and follows the truck driver into the building.

~*~

Once inside, Flynn is confronted by an unsympathetic glare from Camille, beside the billiard table, conversing with the truck driver. She considers the irritated pilot standing in the doorway before taking the clipboard and looking down at the paperwork. Her pen clicks loudly, as she nods her head while reading the shipping documents. She then puts her initials on the margin of the top sheet.

Kicking his foot against the doors to make them slam, Flynn growls, "What the hell do you think you're doing?!?" The surprised trucker turns to the entryway to look at Flynn.

Camille simply glances over, before clicking her pen again and signing off on several more pages. Ignoring the angry stare from the pilot, she hands the driver the clipboard and struts toward Flynn. She casually saunters past him to the door as he grumbles, "What's your problem?"

Camille stops and turns to Flynn. "Who, *me*?"

"Yes *you*, dammit!" He attempts to control his anger. "You think you can just come in here and piecemeal us out?"

She pauses briefly, and then, with attitude, uses both hands to push the double doors open. With a quick glance back at the trucker with the paperwork, she sneers at Flynn. "Mister Russell, I don't have time to explain profit margins to you right now. I have to patch together a failing business."

Camille steps through the screened doors and lets them swing back and slap together. The truck driver follows, speaking aside to Flynn. "Sorry, pal... It's my job to make this pickup." He glances outside toward Camille at his truck, and lowers his voice a bit. "Just met her now, but she seems like a real ball-breaker."

Flynn can't help but let a smile crack at the familiar reference to the businesswoman. He nods and replies, "Yeah, buddy... You don't even know the half of it."

Chapter 12

A mulling assembly of pilots and ground-crew stand in front of the row of hangars, across from the flatbed truck as it loads. The crane arm attached to the trailer groans with strain, as it lifts up the scrap fuselage of an A-26 Invader flying tanker. The detached wings and tail lay in piles beside the truck. From the looks of the crumpled landing gear, tarnished skin, and skeletal remains of the wings, the aircraft appears to have survived a crash-landing some decades prior.

Chuck Strode rubs his open palm around the back of his thick neck and sighs heavily. "Dang... I always thought we would get a chance to put that bird back together again." They watch the crane lower the airframe and rest it on the wooden cradle affixed to the flatbed trailer.

Flynn murmurs, "That was the first time I saw the Old Man crack one up. When he climbed out and walked from that wreck in one piece, I thought he was a god."

From behind them, Chip steps up and stops to watch. A sly, crooked smile appears under his bushy moustache. "How many more wrecks did it take before you realized that gods don't come crashing down from out of the clouds?"

They all become reverently silent as the broken-up, vintage airframe creaks and groans after being released from the sling of the crane. Down the way, the doors of the main office squeak on their hinges momentarily and then slam shut.

51

No one pays any heed, until Camille comes over and clears her throat to get their attention. "*Excuse me*, Gentlemen. I don't want to interrupt all your man-hugs and tear-filled goodbyes, but there is still light in the sky and work that needs doing." She glances at the stack of file folders cradled in her arm.

Flynn looks at her over his shoulder and grimaces. "Some folks just can't appreciate when something is sacred."

Camille reads from the top folder and then looks up at the gathering of pilots and crew. She then stares directly at Flynn and replies to his comment. "And some little boys never seem to grow up. C'mon, Mister Russell... You're next to check-ride on the P-2 today."

Flynn looks to the aircraft, fueled-up and ready to go, at the end of the airstrip. Gazing back to Camille, he sniffs, "Who is the hot-shot expert flying along with me today?"

Camille snaps the folder closed and holds the stack of papers at her side. She looks directly at him. "I am."

Flynn stares at her, until she puts on a derisive grin. Finally, he shrugs his shoulders and mutters aside to his pals. "Well then, I guess I better go and put on my big-boy pants."

Camille hears his remark and attempts not to show her irritation. As she walks past Flynn toward the aircraft, she whispers, "You better be ready to show me a hell of a lot more than just your new pair of big-boy pants."

~*~

Buckled into the pilot's chair, Flynn performs his preflight checklist and warms up the engines. He takes a deep breath and looks over to the doleful individual seated beside him in the copilot position. He notices as she thumbs through the personnel file in her lap while clicking her pen and then makes a series of notations. He leans over to have a peek. "What are you writing in there?"

Glancing over at him, her features remain stoic. "Wouldn't you like to know, Mister Russell?"

"Yes, I would... Keeping secrets isn't nice."

She snorts, "You're one to talk about keeping secrets."

There is an odd, but familiar, hinting of constrained feelings, as the two sit together in the close-quarters of the airplane cockpit. Flynn adjusts the mouthpiece of his headset and speaks to her through the intercom. "I took that job because I had to."

"That's the same reason I divorced you."

"Is it?"

"One of many."

Flynn turns from her and looks out the windshield. "Are you ready to go for a ride?"

"With you I am a reluctant passenger."

"I'll try to make it memorable for you." Refocused on the task of flying, Flynn revs the engines and the airplane slowly rolls forward.

~*~

Several pilots and ground-crewmen watch, as the Neptune P-2 readies for takeoff. The combination piston and jet engine water-bomber plane rolls forward onto the airstrip. Both sets of engines suddenly throttle up, and the aircraft lurches forward for takeoff. The water-bomber races down the airstrip and leaps into the sky.

Chuck watches the uneventful departure and exhales. "He better watch it up there. That gal sure wants to nail him. If he don't keep it on the level, she'll clip his wings."

Frowning and sweeping his moustache from his lip, Chip nods his agreement. "Flynn sure likes to make life hard, and that's the type of gal he can drive completely bonkers."

With an amused giggle, Chuck jokingly responds, "They just love 'im or hate 'im, don't they?"

They watch the water-bombing aircraft bank over the trees toward the distant mountains and gradually fly away. Chip rubs under his nose and lets out a melancholy groan. "Usually they end up hating him..."

Chuck nods and adds, "Ain't it the way with 'em all?"

Chapter 13

Flying the Neptune P-2, Flynn looks down at the ridge of mountains and the valley below. He studies the service road cutting through the trees and snaking through the wooded terrain. Looking over at his certified passenger, he sees her studying the observer checklist which is conspicuously turned away from his view. "So, what's first on that list of yours?"

Camille looks over at him, while she adjusts the arm of the microphone on her headset. The radio crackles, and her voice comes through... cold and practical. "Let's do some low-level flying to evaluate your comfort level with it."

Flynn cracks an amused grin and then glances over at her. "Low-flying comfort level... Are you kidding?"

Camille's professional demeanor remains unaffected as she holds her clipboard at the ready while clicking the pen in her hand. "Mister Russell... I'm not here to be making jokes." As if reading right from the official training procedure form, Camille continues, "Proficiency at low-level flying is a key skill for effectiveness in dousing a targeted fire from the air and in aiding the ground-crew during a surface burn."

Tapping a finger to the brim of his cap, Flynn shrugs and pushes the yoke forward into a steep dive. The engines whine from the rapid descent, and the treetops race toward them. Holding her clipboard tightly, Camille is pushed back into her seat and tries to remain outwardly calm despite the gut-wrenching plunge.

Just before the aircraft nose-dives into the forest floor, Flynn pulls back hard on the yoke and skims the airplane just above the trees. Keeping the water-bomber low on the deck, the wingtips almost slash through the timbered landscape. The pilot grins and looks over at his reserved passenger. "How's this for tree-top flying?"

"A bit extreme... But, satisfactory."

With the practiced skill of an aerobatic stunt pilot, Flynn maneuvers the aircraft under a hundred feet altitude. Unsatisfied with her passive response, he dips the airplane even lower, and the expanse of trees swishes by beneath them. A lone pine tree juts up, higher than the rest, and Flynn banks the wing to swerve around it, barely avoiding a collision. Camille grumbles snidely, "If you hit a tree, you lose points."

The engines roar, as the airplane banks away and levels out. Back on course, Flynn frowns at his unshaken passenger. "You had enough low-level flying yet?"

Camille looks at him with a flaccid expression and nods. "That's fine, if it's the best you can do."

Still buzzing low along the treetops, Flynn glances over to the empty, two lane service road, cut through the forest. Suddenly, a mischievous twinkle appears in his eyes, which is often a telling sign of his lesser thought-out notions. Gripping the yoke, he mutters into the microphone on his headset. "Want to get a lower perspective?"

Camille glimpses questioningly at the stunt-flyer, just as Flynn turns the yoke and dives the airplane down toward the roadway. "What are you doing...?"

Dropping into the narrow cut between the trees, Flynn flies the fire-bombing airplane twenty feet off the pavement. The ride-along passenger stares at the aviator with a stern countenance that lacks any sort of juvenile amusement. Despite the tree trunks flashing by at eye-level, Camille pronounces to Flynn, "Who's the joker now?"

The pilot grins with satisfaction and gradually pulls the airplane up over the tree line. Flynn looks at the clipboard braced against Camille's lap as she writes, and he questions, "What else ya got there on your checklist?"

Pointed north by northwest, the airplane continues to climb to a higher altitude before finally leveling off in flight. Suddenly, there is a rattling clank, followed by a violent shudder and explosion that is felt throughout the airframe. Flynn's eyes dart to the gauges on the panel before he looks out the windows at the dark smoke starting to billow from both of the right engines. He mutters under his breath, "Shit..."

The examiner looks out her near window at the idly whirling propeller alongside the smoldering jet engine. Orange licks of flames and a trailing cloud of black smoke stream back from the cowling of the engines. Camille turns to look at the pilot and points out to the wing. "Uh, Flynn... There are flames!"

He shuts down the fuel supply to the damaged engines and quickly assesses their dilemma. "I see 'em..." In a wide, smoke-trailing turn, he banks the compromised airplane to fly back toward the Fire Angel airbase. Pulling back on the yoke, he states calmly through the radio, "Okay... Heading home."

Powered by the remaining engines, the airplane levels out, and Flynn stares ahead at the ridge of trees directly before them. A mountain seems to rise up before them as they continue to fly nearer. Glancing at Camille, Flynn speaks through the intercom. "We need to gain a bit more altitude to make it over that ridge." He looks over at her and smiles.

"Would you mind terribly if we skipped ahead on the checklist to the part where I drop this payload?"

Camille turns her attention away from the approaching ridge-line and can hardly believe that his he is joking about their dire situation. "Yes, drop it!"

Flynn pulls the flaps to little effect. "Where would you like me to put it?"

She stares ahead toward an imminent collision, should they maintain their current altitude. "Flynn, I don't give a damn where it goes! *Just drop it!*"

"Okay! See that tree down there?" Flynn jabs a finger over the instrument panel. "The one crooked out to the east, next to the bigger one... I think it's a Western White Pine."

She looks over at him in shock. "Just *do it*, before we hit that mountain!"

Barely above the treetops, the plane zooms toward the mountainside. Flynn moves his hand over to the water-bombing controls, hesitates, and then releases the payload from the drop tanks. A plume of water cascades from the belly of the air-tanker, and the remaining operable engines respond by pulling the aircraft higher above the tree line.

The showering mist of water cascades over the trees, and the aircraft buzzes over the high ridge so that the fliers look out at the distant valley below. Camille audibly lets out a held breath while still gripping her clipboard to her lap. Behind the controls, the relieved pilot looks at her impishly. "You're not going to take note of that awesome water drop?"

She looks over at him and rolls her eyes in reply. "Just keep flying the plane, Mister Russell."

The Fire Angel airbase comes into view on the floor of the next valley, nested between forested hillsides. Flynn looks past his passenger to the wing with the flamed-out engines, as smoke continues to waft behind the wind-milling propeller.

Fire Angels

"Flying planes is what I do best. All the way to the ground…"
He grins smugly, as he adjusts the tail rudder to counteract
the adverse yaw of the functioning engines on the one side.

Chapter 14

The sound of a struggling airplane trailing smoke across the sky gets everyone's attention at the airbase. Several pilots and ground-crew from various buildings come running out to the runway, readying for an emergency landing. Someone climbs into the water truck and starts it up to power the pumps.

Frederick Thompson bursts through the screen doors of the main building and hollers orders into a radio handset. "Chip... Get that fuel tanker cleared away from the runway!" With the crowd, he walks briskly toward the cleared landing strip while looking up to the gradually descending aircraft. Woody comes jogging up alongside him, matching his pace, and adjusts his ball cap. "Is that Flynn bringing in the P-2?"

The old man glances aside and responds, "Yep."

"Doing a check-ride?"

"Yep..."

Woody hurries a bit to keep in step. "Who's he with?" Frederick takes a deep breath, then replies, "She is."

The pilot gulps hard and murmurs, "Ahh, shit..."

~*~

The smell of burnt oil and the rumbling from the last pair of engines make for a loud and uncomfortable cockpit. Flynn adjusts the fuel mixture to maximize their power and lines the aircraft up to approach the Fire Angel landing strip. Looking over at his passenger, he can't help but smile.

Still clutching the clipboard in her lap, Camille stares out the front windscreen. As they quickly approach the airbase, she peers past Flynn to the engines on the wing, then back at the pilot. "I know you're a good flyer, Flynn."

Occupied with the damaged aircraft emergency landing procedure, Flynn gives her a quick nodding smile and then humorously gestures at her tightly held clipboard. "Yep... Before we crash, write that down above the rest of it."

Camille shakes her head, not even slightly amused, and mutters. "It's the only thing you were ever really good at."

Turning his full attention to look at her, Flynn puts on an expression of hurt pride and responds, "Come on... *Really?* There were *other* things, weren't there?"

Her jaw clenched tight, Camille jabs a finger ahead in the direction of the landing strip. "Keep flying the airplane, Mister Russell."

Flynn gives her a deliberate wink and glibly adds, "Well, you know us cocky flyers... Always like to finish hard and with a flourish!" He returns to the controls and studies their fixed approach. The whole frame of the airplane shudders, as the last of the engines power them toward the airstrip below.

~*~

The P-2 Neptune fire-bomber approaches the landing field at a steady airspeed, canted slightly to the strong side. The power-challenged aircraft hovers over the flight strip momentarily and then finally completes a by-the-book, three-point landing that makes use of the entire length of runway. Everyone admiringly watches the accomplished landing and then, simultaneously, all seem to let out a held breath of air. Frederick looks aside to Woody and then touches under his own jawline for a pulse. "Dammit anyhow... I thought I was having a heart attack." He takes a deep breath and murmurs, "Good boy, Flynn."

Unscathed by the emergency landing, the airplane taxies to the end of the airstrip and turns toward the hangars. After the remaining pair of engines propels the aircraft the short distance, Flynn then cuts the power, leaving a silent whirl of a single propeller. Watching the aircraft come to a safe stop, Frederick composes himself and, all business again, turns to speak with Woody. "Get Wing Nut and his crew to find out what happened and then overhaul those two engines. Fire season is upon us, so we need every set of wings we got."

Snapping an obedient salute, Woody shuffles off to the hangar, and Frederick turns to walk back to the office. Halting outside the doors of the main building, he considers the recent event and quietly reflects on the consequences. He silently watches the rotating propeller, until it finally spins to a halt. Taking a calming breath, he passes through the double doors.

~*~

The rear hatch door on the P-2 Neptune swings open, and Camille climbs out with her clipboard and pen in hand. She starts to walk away, as Flynn appears in the opening and calls after her. "Hey Vanderhaus! How'd I do?"

She stops, hesitates, and then turns to look up at him. "You did just fine… Other than that roadway incident."

He smiles at her and leans forward out of the hatch. "Aww, darlin'… That was just what you ordered to demonstrate my low-level flying skills."

Camille nods stiffly. "Try to keep those low-life tendencies at bay from now on, if you continue to fly with us."

Riled at her icy tone, Flynn can't help but respond. "You know, I'd rather be a low-life than to be wound so tight as to have no life at all."

Tucking her clipboard under her arm, Camille stares up at Flynn. She clenches her jaw and speaks sternly. "Let's keep this professional, Mister Russell."

Flynn lets the dour expression drop and nods. "Yeah... You got it, *Sir*. Professional all the way..." He watches Camille turn on a heel and march along the landing strip to the office. Ducking back inside the aircraft, he grumbles to himself. "Screw it... I guess neither one of us has changed much."

Chapter 15

At the edge of the town nearest the air base, just off the main road, is a lodge-style eating establishment with a sign on the roof which reads: *The Air-Drop Coffee Shop.* Parked in front, beside an old pickup truck, is Flynn's mud-spattered vehicle. The sky above the treetops is clear and blue, but strong gusts of wind blow intermittently, bending over the tips of the tallest evergreens.

Bellied-up to the uncrowded breakfast counter, Flynn and Chip each have a steaming cup of coffee set before them. The mustached pilot takes a testing sip and uses his napkin to dab away the wetness from his overhanging lip-whiskers. "That was a hell of a ride you gave the lady-suit today."

Flynn wraps his hand around his mug and smiles. "Any landing everyone can walk away from is the good one."

Unamused, Chip shakes his head and tilts his chin toward Flynn. "No bullshit here. The Old Man is more than a little worried that he's gonna lose the whole operation before the season even starts."

The grin fades from Flynn's face, and he takes a drink from his coffee. "Yeah, he's been looking pretty down."

They both stare ahead to the mirror, mounted behind the meal counter, which reflects the view of an awe-inspiring panorama of forested mountain terrain. Chip swipes his forefinger under his bushy moustache. "Dang, this ain't the same business it was when I got into it several decades ago." He hunches his shoulders and reminisces. "I was working crop-dusters with my dad at eleven, soloed at fourteen, and was bush-flying all over Alaska in my twenties. Did you know I had my own flight charter out of Aspen for a while?"

Gazing past his own reflection in the mirror to the stunning landscape outside Flynn asks, "What happened with the charter service?"

"Just ran its course… Like all things seem to do in life. Sold out to the bigger operations and moved on to this…"

They both feel the pangs of uneasiness regarding the changing times ahead. Flynn queries, "Ever wish you didn't sell and held out longer?"

"Nope. Not at all… Those companies were better-funded and brought in newer aircraft, which I couldn't compete with. Was only a matter of time before it was out with the old and in with the new. I figured it was a good time to move on while I could still get something out of it."

The waitress approaches from behind the counter, freshens Chip's coffee and smiles at the two regular customers. "Hello, fellas. You guys gonna want something other than just coffee today?"

They look over to the pastry display case and Flynn considers the contents. "Why don't you bring us one of those frosted, cinnamon sweet-rolls along with two donuts."

Chip shakes his head. "Nothing for me, thanks."

The waitress looks at Chip and then back to Flynn. "The bakery items are just for you then?"

"Yeah, but spread it out on some plates. It looks bad if you stack it up in front of me. He'll change his mind anyway."

Eyebrow raised, Chip humorously gazes over at Flynn and then back to the waitress. "Bring me some eggs and bacon." He smirks at Flynn and laughs. "For show, that is."

Fire Angels

The waitress shakes her head at the familiar jokesters and reaches out the pot of coffee to refresh Flynn's coffee cup. "I don't know what we're gonna do when we don't have you colorful characters coming around anymore."

Flynn acts surprised. "Why would we stop coming?" Suddenly, the waitress looks stunned, like she spoke out of turn. "Oh, sorry... I must have misheard."

Chip crinkles his brow. "What did you mishear?"

"Oh... Well, uh, everyone is talking about the new management arriving to liquidate the air base."

Flynn and Chip exchange a troubled glance but don't look too terribly shocked at the news. Simultaneously, they lift their coffee cups up. Before Flynn takes a sip, he murmurs, "We aren't gone just yet."

Chip swallows his gulp of coffee and replies, "Nope... Not yet."

Feeling somewhat uncomfortable, the waitress tops off Chip's mug before scooting away to the pastry display to gather their orders. Flynn watches her and then glances to Chip. "Well, what do you think about that?"

"She probably ain't wrong."

Flynn nods and gazes into his steaming cup of brew. "How long do you think we got?"

The mustached pilot chews on his lip and mutters, "This season, or maybe the next. You've been doing the right thing with picking up freelance work in Arizona."

"I just need to be up in the air."

With both hands wrapped around the hot cup of coffee, Chip stares forward at their reflections in the mirror. He looks to the streaks of silver on his head and his grey facial hair. Almost apologetically, he mutters. "This will probably be my last season doing this."

Surprised, Flynn looks up from staring at his coffee. "Why? There are other outfits out there looking to hire."

"Yeah, but this was a good one, and I'd rather leave on my own terms than end up begging for a job behind the stick, or being shit-canned by an uppity airline."

Thinking on it a while, and Flynn adds, "I don't know. It seems the fire season stretches longer each year and good pilots don't just happen overnight."

Chip puts his coffee down and, with a friendly smile, turns his head toward Flynn. "They won't need any of us experienced flyers much longer. Someday, they'll just need someone to push the buttons."

"There is no shortcut to experience."

Chip snorts his agreement and bemoans, "You know, folks like us get off on flying these archaic war crates. The next generation coming up can hardly comprehend an actual world-war happening, let alone Korea or Vietnam." He lifts his coffee mug to take another sip and continues. "Sometimes, I even find it amazing that we're still flying airplanes that were built almost a half century ago."

"Not everyone can afford the newer conversions."

Smoothing his moustache aside, Chip nods grimly. "The ones that stay in business can or won't be in it long."

The two friends are quiet for a moment, until the waitress returns with Flynn's big breakfast of donuts and a sweet-roll. She spreads the items out in front of the two pilots and smiles. "Here ya go. Eggs will be right up."

They nod their thanks, as the waitress leaves and Flynn peeks inquisitively over at Chip. "What do ya think of that suit they sent over to be in charge?"

Chip catches the quick, inquiring look. After taking a short sip of coffee, he mutters, "Seems just like your type."

68

Fire Angels

Coughing up a bit of donut, Flynn exclaims, "Yeah...?!? What type is that, exactly?"

The mustached pilot gives a laugh and cradles his beverage with two hands. "A real ball-bustin' *you-know-what*." He looks at the old friend beside him and curiously adds, "You know her from somewhere before?"

Flynn clears his throat, takes a quick breath, and replies. "Yeah... *Some*, but mostly by reputation."

Chapter 16

Standing outside the Fire Angel Aviation hangar that has the PBY Catalina seaplane inside, Flynn watches as a forklift crew loads salvaged airplane pieces and crates of miscellaneous parts into the cargo hold of another semi-truck. Wing Nut steps up beside Flynn and puts a consoling hand on his shoulder. "Try not to worry too much about that stuff, buddy. The Old Man was a real junk-hoarder, and those things there were mostly useless to us for our current fleet."

They watch, as the pallets of materials are lifted into the container and then tucked away. Flynn clenches his jaw. "Some warbird collector has hit the jackpot this year."

Adjusting his cap, Wing Nut nods and then steps away. "Well, don't start shitting bricks until she sends over one of her junior-assistants to take photos of the Catalina."

Flynn nods and continues to observe the clearing out of the neighboring hangar. A pulsing vibration in his pocket signals a message on his pager, and he is about to take a look when Kansas Sam jogs out of the hangar directly behind him. The pilot heads for the main office and calls over his shoulder. "We just got the contract on a burner out near Ketchum. They're putting the crews together now."

Looking down at the phone number on his pager, Flynn recognizes the Fire Angel digits, and tucks it away as he follows Sam toward the office. "Right behind you pard..."

~*~

Inside the office command post, the crew of pilots stands around one of the large conference tables with a map spread open on its surface. Standing a bit behind the group, Camille, clipboard in-hand, observes and takes notes on each member of the aerial firefighter crew. Most of the pilots remain oblivious to her presence, but Flynn gives her an occasional glance, keenly aware that she is watching.

As usual, Frederick performs the role of base manager and points out the positions of each hot spot. He waves his hand over the terrain and jabs a stout finger toward the upper corner of the topography map, laying out the plan of attack. "We have strong winds coming in from the north-west, and the strongest burn is moving toward Hailey." The pilots all lean in to study map, while their leader continues his briefing. "With the forecast of sporadic winds that could be coming from the south in a few days, they want this fire contained before it poses a threat to homes in Ketchum and Sun Valley. As it is, the governor's office is getting calls about local air quality and what they're doing about it."

Kansas Sam looks over his dark sunshades and speaks up jokingly. "You want me to go over there with the chopper and clear smoke away from the rich people's homes in town?"

Chuck pipes in, "Kansas, you don't even *need* the chopper, with all the hot air you can blow."

Sam grinningly retorts, "Who do you think blows up all your birthday balloons?"

Chuck laughs. "I thought it was some other clown."

There are a few lighthearted chuckles, until Camille clears her throat to remind them of her constant presence. Flynn stands with his arms crossed and watches the effect she has on moral. Frederick glances over his shoulder at her, and then gets back to business. "With these winds and the amount of smoke and debris in the air, we will be going in with a lead plane first to determine the angle of attack." He looks around at his pilot crew. "Chuck, I want you up front in the Bronco with an eye on everything to keep us informed here at base." His gaze steadily moves around to each of them, as he begins to assign positions. "Chip and Sam… Take the chopper and the Bambi Bucket. You should be able to get plenty of water from the river." He traces his hand across the area and looks up at Flynn. "Since the P-2 is out of service for the time being, I want you and Woody to take the Catalina…"

There is a cough from behind, and Camille speaks out. "No…" With questioning expressions, everyone turns to look at her. Without lowering her clipboard, she gestures Frederick aside for a private meeting. The two supervisors move over to the Old Man's desk by the observation windows, and their terse conversation is only partly overheard by the flyers.

After a short, heated discussion, they finish and return to the conference table. Frederick looks at his crew of airmen. His eyes connect with Flynn's a moment then he looks away. He puts his hands to the table and grumbles, "The Catalina stays here. Flynn, take the Douglas DC-3 with Floyd."

Everyone pauses, holding their breath while avoiding any immediate eye contact. Woody looks around timidly, then leans forward over the map and looks directly at the Old Man. He clears his throat before asking what everyone is thinking. "Well, what about me?" The stillness in the room is deafening. "You want me to take up the Fire Boss on this one?"

There is an uncomfortable moment of silence, until Frederick finally responds, "No… You're grounded for now. Stick around after the briefing. We need to have a talk. Everyone else, get your aircraft loaded and be ready to fly."

A feeling of uncertainty fills the room, as the pilots slowly shuffle downstairs and exit the building. Flynn looks to the Old Man but only gets a distracted shrug. A communal sense of dread hangs heavy in the air, as the fire-fighters see bad news coming for one of their own. Eventually, everyone in the main office has cleared out with the exception of Frederick, Camille and Woody.

Chapter 17

With Chip at the controls, the chopper with the Bambi bucket lifts off the helipad in a swirl of debris and dust-filled air. Across the airfield, the belching roar of twin radial engines erupts, as the propellers of the DC-3 slowly begin to rotate. Gradually making its way toward the runway, the OV-10A Bronco taxies and prepares for its takeoff.

Several members of the ground-crew stand by, as the small fleet of fire-bombing aircraft departs for their mission. The Bronco races down the runway, nimbly lifts into the air and banks to the west. Inside the DC-3, Flynn slides his side window closed and looks over at Floyd in the copilot chair. "You ready to put some smoke through your wings?"

"A big ten-four on that, pal."

The wheel brakes release with a squeaking groan, and the aircraft begins to taxi forward. Flynn steers the airplane with the tail rudder and sings out, "Here we go into the wild blue yonder..."

Hovering in the sky above the base, the fire-chopper flies with a deflated water-drop contraption dangling below. It lifts higher and then pivots to follow after the departing Bronco aircraft, as the larger tanker turns onto the runway. With Flynn at the controls of the DC-3, it powers up, blowing back billowing clouds of dust and dry grass. The fire-bombing tanker charges down the air strip and slowly lifts into the sky.

On the horizon, the fire-chopper follows after the lead plane, and the air tanker banks its wings, bringing up the rear.

~*~

The skies over Ketchum, Idaho are marred by a pillar of smoke drifting to the south in the direction of the oncoming aircraft. Flying from clear skies into a murky grey firmament, the fire-bombing aircraft cut through the dense haze of smoke. Ahead, the glowing-orange flash of flames can be seen spreading across the wilderness landscape.

~*~

Inside the Bronco, Chuck maneuvers the airplane through the smoke-filled air, as drifting bits of hot ash fleck off the windscreen. He adjusts the headset microphone and speaks into the communications radio. "Bronco-One here... Why don't you guys spill off to clearer skies on the flank, so we can get a handle on how big this is and where it's going."

The radio crackles noisily, until Flynn's voice responds. "Copy that... We'll circle east in the Douglas, and Chip will fly the whirlybird in clearer skies to the west to get water."

Chuck pushes his sunglasses up higher on his nose. "Affirmative... I'll make the initial pass and scout out the route of attack."

The radio cuts out, and then Chip's voice breaks in. "Copy that Bronco... Off to fill the Bambi bucket."

Large glowing embers continue to drift upward, tinking off the fuselage and glass windshield of the leading aircraft, as Chuck flies closer to the forest fire raging below. The orange flecks whirl through the spinning propellers like fireflies through an electric egg beater. Straining to see through the smoke and ash, he dives the aircraft toward the flaming treetops.

~*~

Fire Angels

From the cockpit of the DC-3, Flynn watches the twin-engine Bronco charge through the thick cloud of smoke and then disappear from sight. Only the muffled sound of engines can be heard, as the lead plane charges in low over the burning landscape. He looks to the clearer skies in the west and watches the chopper with the dangling water bucket fly to the reservoir. Flynn glances over at Floyd and comments. "We're in it now, buddy..." The DC-3 circles around the rising column of smoke, flying counter-clockwise to cut through the peripheral haze as the hot, dense currents of air rise from the blazing fire below.

Suddenly, from the orange, glowing cloud, the Bronco emerges from the other side of the smoldering pillar of smoke. Chuck breathes a sigh of relief as his plane, with rolling wisps of smoke clinging to the tail section and wingtips, frees itself from the clutches of the wildfire. As he clicks his radio on, Chuck coughs and swats at the foggy haze inside the cockpit. "Bronco-One here... The central burn is traveling south by southwest with intermittent heavy wind gusts." He pulls up, climbing higher as he banks the airplane away from the fire. In the distance, he sees the helicopter lifting from the river with a full water bucket. Scanning around, Chuck tries to get a visual on the larger water-bomber, while he continues to speak into the radio. "There is a line of canyons due east. Stopping the blaze along the ridgeline will create a nice fire-break for anything trying to sweep toward Sun Valley."

Chuck tilts his gaze overhead, as the DC-3 thunders past him. He watches as the larger airplane circles around to come up alongside him. As the two aircrafts fly in formation, Flynn's voice comes on the receiver. "Copy that, Bronco-One. We have eyes on the ridge and will follow you to come around and carry out our approach from the south."

Eric H. Heisner

A muffled voice comes through the radio, and Chip confirms his readiness and position. "I'm on your six, fellas, and will follow you in…"

Chapter 18

The DC-3 firebomber banks around the rising smoke. Approaching from the south, the aircraft moves into position to target the fire below. Flynn glances over to see Floyd Fisher kicked-back and relaxing while reading a book. "What are you reading there, Fish?"

The Fish lowers his paperback and looks over at Flynn. "Oh, just some mushy romance-novel thing."

The large aircraft's engines roar, as it comes around in line with the fiery ridge. Flynn grips the controls and gazes ahead, as he chats casually with his copilot. "Is it any good?"

"It's okay..." Fisher puts on his best Scottish accent. "You know, one of those ladies-love-kilts sorts of things."

Flynn laughs and smiles in reply. "Gals just trying to find out what's worn under there?"

The copilot, with his signature lopsided-grin, retorts, "Just tell the ladies, there is nothing *worn* under there... Though, it is used quite a bit!" Looking at the flaming landscape ahead, the quirky flyer giggles as he marks the page in his book and tosses the paperback novel over his shoulder. "Okay... Time to go to work?"

The airplane jolts in the warm updrafts. While holding the controls firm in spite of the increasing turbulence, Flynn nods as he replies, "Yep... Time to earn our pay."

Through the cockpit windows, they witness the orange licks of flame engulfing the trees below. Floyd focuses on his copilot duties and instantly transforms from a wise-cracking goofball into a serious aerial fire-fighter. As they descend, the gusting updrafts, full of embers, violently jostle the airplane.

~*~

The Douglas DC-3 charges over the raging wildfire. They veer to the right and line up on the canyon ridge, just to the flank of the surface burn. Racing over the treetops, the fire-fighting air tanker rumbles through gusting winds filled with hot ash and heavy smoke. Licks of fire reach up through the woodland canopy and reflect off the polished metal skin of the low-flying plane. Directly above the target, the water-bomber drops its payload along the high ridge of the canyon. Over the roar of engines, the dump of water and fire-retardant creates a swishing-hiss that quenches some of the fire below.

Fish peers out his side window to the blanketed path and howls a yipping, coyote-like scream, followed by exclaiming, "Right on target there, buddy-boy!!"

Flynn pulls back on the yoke, and the big water-bomber roars up and away from the flame-engulfed treetops. He wipes beads of sweat from his brow, adjusts his lucky cap under the headset and clicks the radio. "Big Douglas here… We dropped our load on the ridge and are en route to temp base to refill for another."

Chuck's voice crackles through the static on the radio. "Good drop boys! Keep 'em coming."

The DC-3 climbs out and away from the billowing cloud of smoke to clearer skies above. Flynn looks out his side window over to the chopper swinging it's water-filled Bambi-bucket toward the leading edge of the wildfire. Where a road cuts through the wilderness below, Flynn can see multiple fire-fighting vehicles unloading crews to work along the forward lines. He clicks his microphone on. "Be advised that there are ground-crews forming-up along the forest access road to the south. A bucket drop to their heading will be much appreciated."

From the chopper, Chip's voice responds, "Copy that. Please confirm Bronco-One?"

Chuck clicks on, "That's affirmative."

The radio chatter crackles, as the DC-3 flies away to get refilled and the chopper drops into the smoky haze. Above the burn site, the Bronco circles the column of smoke, supervising the execution of the water drops.

~*~

Several days later, at the Fire Angels headquarters near Pocatello, the DC-3 fire-bombing tanker roars over the airstrip. Buzzing the main building, the large aircraft banks over the trees at the end of the valley to come around again for a landing. The smoke and ash-tarnished airplane drops in over the landing field and puts down on its two front wheels using a surprisingly short stretch of runway. Inside the cockpit, Flynn Russell is positioned behind the controls, steering the plane toward the row of the hangars. As he nears the wide-open doors, one of the radial engines revs louder, and the airplane pivots on the braked wheel under the opposite wing. Clouds of dust and grassy debris blow back from the throttled-up engine until the power is cut on both engines, and they chug to a halt.

The rear hatch of the DC-3 opens, and Floyd the Fish jumps out to the ground, ducking under the broad wing to grab a pair of tire chocks for each of the forward wheels. Flynn looks outside the hatch before climbing down with his bag. He looks across the air base to the Bronco airplane parked nearby and the helicopter settled on the grassy landing pad.

He peeks under the wing and hollers to Floyd. "Thanks, Fish, I'll see you at *The Dump*."

The copilot gives an affirming wave and goes back to his visual inspection of the exterior of the workhorse plane. "Yeah buddy... See you over there in a bit."

With duffle in hand, Flynn walks the path to the main building and pulls open one of the double screen doors.

Chapter 19

Several of the recently returned fire-pilots gather at the back of the old-west styled Fire Angels recreation room known as *The Dump*. Flynn lets the screen doors swing shut behind him and tosses his duffle bag to an empty tabletop. He struts over to join his friends at the bar and looks to the vacant shelves that once carried various types of alcohol. "Not having a bar stocked properly should be a punishable crime." He shakes his head with disappointment and bellies up to the bar with the rest of them.

Behind the bar, Kansas Sam uses his shirt tail to polish his mirrored sunshades before slipping them back on. "Flynn, what can I get for you?"

"What have you got?"

Sam laughs and winks. "Just soda pop."

Flynn looks down the bar at everyone's beverages and then back to the host bartender to see if he's actually joking. Kansas Sam lifts a bottle of liquor from concealment behind the bar. The bartender swishes the contraband alcohol and grins. "With a little something extra, of course..."

Delighted, Flynn nods. "Okay, give me one of those." As Kansas Sam mixes up a special drink for him, Flynn looks down the bar to Chip and Chuck, who each drink from a matching, cowboy-style tin cup. He turns to look around the room and asks, "Where's Woody?" Chip sucks his lower lip in under his moustache and stares ahead to the empty shelves behind the bar. He doesn't reply, and Chuck merely looks into his cup, until Flynn finally asks, "What happened?"

Chuck looks at Flynn, shaking his head mournfully. "Bad news... They clipped his wings 'n grounded him."

"Why?" Flynn looks around to the others for answers, as Sam slides him a soda pop cocktail in a tin cup.

Taking another swallow from his drink, Chuck clears his throat and replies to Flynn. "Guess he didn't measure up to what the skirt upstairs expects from us."

"Dammit..." Lifting the cup to his lips, Flynn takes a long drink and then has an irrepressible shiver from the taste. He looks at Sam, who merely gives him an innocent grin. "Hey Kansas, is there even any soda pop in here?"

Sam shrugs. "I never said it was a real fancy cocktail. Just figured I could stretch a can of soda a good ways."

Flynn lifts his cup for a toast. "To a job well done..." The others at the bar raise their tin cups as well, while Flynn continues the respectful tribute. "... and to our pal, Woody." The pilots clank their cups together then take swallows. Silently reverent, they all stare into their drinks until Flynn asks the obvious. "Where is he?"

Kansas Sam drops a few cubes of ice into his cup and pours himself another drink. He lifts his leg onto a stool behind the bar. "Wing Nut told me he took a few days off to consider his options."

Swirling the mixture in his cup, Flynn shakes his head. "Options... What are his options?"

Chuck absentmindedly taps a finger on the handle of his metal cup and murmurs, "Supposedly, they offered him a job with the ground-crew if he wants it."

Pondering a moment, Flynn replies, "Why doesn't he just get a flying gig somewhere else?"

Fire Angels

Chip tips his cup back, swallows the last of his drink and then wipes his moustache. "Not many folks looking to hire an aged pilot after he was grounded from his last gig."

Mulling it over, Flynn mutters, "The Old Man would give someone another chance, if they had the right stuff and were to ask for it."

Pushing his empty cup away, Chip leans over to look down the bar at his fellow pilots and then lets his gaze linger on Flynn. "We're at the end of the line for that kind of thing. That skirt upstairs is gonna drag us into the new, updated world of aviation, where the antiques are polished up to be put on static display, and the old junk is discarded."

Sam clanks his drink down on the bar top and groans, "We might as well go 'n get a haircut, put on a docent frock, and get a job at the local Air Park Museum."

After taking a few more drinks, Flynn begins to feel the effect of the alcohol. Then, that familiar sensation of irritation and frustration brought on by Camille Vanderhaus creeps in. He stares at the empty shelves and looks over at his friends. Fed up with it all, he slaps his hand on the bar and growls. "This is damn bullshit!"

Surprised at Flynn's sudden reaction, Chip tilts his head and states, "Nothing to be done about it. That's just the way it is now."

The two old friends exchange a look of understanding, and Flynn thinks to their recent conversation about retiring. "You know… I think that someone with Woody's years of experience deserves better that to be just put out to pasture."

Sweeping a finger by his moustache, Chip murmurs, "*Deserves* really got nothing to do with it." The rest of the group remains quiet. Flynn shoves his drink away and looks at the set of stairs leading up to the office.

Tilting his cup, Chuck rolls the bottom edge on the bar. "We all know what you're feeling buddy, but it won't help anything to get in her face about it."

As he steps away from the bar and marches to the stairs, Flynn loudly grumbles, "Maybe not... But, it will make me feel a whole helluva lot better."

Chip leans an elbow on the bar and watches the infuriated aviator climb the stairway. He raises an eyebrow and shakes his head dolefully. "You'll get yourself crossways with her and not get any satisfaction."

Stopping to peer over the hand rail, Flynn calls back, "Telling her what's-what is all the satisfaction *I* need!"

Chapter 20

Flynn stomps up the set of wooden stairs to announce his arrival to the upper office. He turns the corner after the top step and notices the Old Man at the big desk by the window and Camille speaking on the phone at another workspace. Marching over to stop at the center of the room, he glares at Camille. Frederick puts an elbow to his desk and runs his hand through his silver hair. He recognizes the look on Flynn's face and realizes that a storm is brewing. "Can I help you with something?"

Staring daggers at Camille, Flynn jabs a finger in her direction as she continues her conversation on the telephone. "I want to have a talk with her."

Camille's eyes flit upward to the pilot, and she turns back to her telephone call. Flynn continues his firm stance, until she finally reacts and switches the phone to her other ear. "I'll have to call you back. Something has come up." Unhurried, she hangs up the phone receiver, shuffles some papers on her table and then finally swivels her chair to face the noticeably upset pilot. "Mister Russell, is there something troubling you?"

"Damn-straight there is! You know what..."

Waiting patiently for Flynn to continue, Camille and Frederick stare back at him, but he seems too exasperated to find the right words. She turns to look at the papers on her desk and begins to casually shuffle through them again. Fuming, he continues to stare at her until she looks up at him. Her eyes widen, and she sarcastically utters, "Am I supposed to guess what is on your mind?"

"Garrison Pyle."

Camille puts down the stack of papers and focuses her attention on Flynn. "Oh, so you are referring to *Woody*." Flynn nods his head, and the Old Man leans back in his creaking desk chair to observe the confrontation. Remaining seated, Camille responds in a matter-of-fact way. "He is on leave, taking a few days off to consider things."

"That's exactly what I just found out."

"So, what's the problem? He hasn't been fired."

Flynn clenches his jaw and almost spits his words. "What I *heard* was... You took his wings away!"

Camille slowly pushes her chair back from the table, repositions her crossed legs and takes a slip of paper from the corner of her desk. She glances down at it for a moment and then returns her gaze to the livid pilot. "He has only ten percent vision in his right eye. The other one is at eighty and will mostly likely decline as well."

"What are you talking about?"

She holds out the slip of paper to Flynn. He takes it and reads the stationary header for an eye institute in Boise. Camille gives him a few moments to look over the report and then speaks. "The degenerative eye condition has been present for a couple of years, but I guess he has pretty much managed to hide it from everyone... Until now." Camille continues, as Flynn scans the details of the doctor's report. "After having a look at everyone's personnel file, I noticed more than a few minor incidents, which, on the surface, seemed to be only trivial occurrences. After flying with him, I had him submitted for a complete physical examination, and that is what they found."

"Doesn't he deserve a chance to get a second opinion before you clip his wings?"

Looking over at Frederick and then to Flynn again, she shakes her head. "This came as no surprise to Mister Pyle."

Flynn drops the report back on her table and stares down at Camille. "You flew with him. He's a talented flyer. Let him finish out this fire season, and he can retire after."

A spark of an old irritation ignites in Camille's eyes. She pushes her chair back and stands before him. "Excuse me, Mister Russell... You may think this all a fun sport in your boys club of tree-top flyers, but I am trying to save what is left of this so-called business!"

"Let the man have his pride!"

"Pride won't keep him alive."

"It isn't much of a life without it!"

Facing-off with Flynn, her gaze seems to bore right through him. "If you want to get shit-faced and throw a retirement party for your old flying pal, then go right ahead. He's not safe to go up and fly one of our airplanes!"

Looking away from her, Flynn mutters, under his breath, "You cold-hearted..."

Camille can't help but raise her voice at him in reply. "Go ahead... Finish that thought! It won't change anything."

He turns to her, and then he glances back to where his supervisor sits discreetly at his desk. Outside the big window, the sky is darkening with an approaching storm. Flustered, Flynn shakes his head at his friend and mentor. "Old Man, I don't think you would have handled it this way before she came around."

Frederick solemnly stares at Flynn. "There is nothing to do but offer him a job on the ground."

"You know that is no kind of life for a flyer."

"We all have it coming eventually."

Flynn turns to leave, and Camille calls after him. "Mister Pyle understood and had the foresight to see that his days of flying were numbered at least. It would be wise for you *all* to look to your *own* futures.",Flynn halts in his tracks, clenches his jaw and thinks for a moment, before he walks away without responding. Descending the stairway, he casts one last glance back, before murmuring something unintelligible as he disappears from sight.

Chapter 21

The double screen doors to the main building burst open, and Flynn steps out with his flight duffle in hand. He looks up to the dark storm clouds blowing overhead and deeply inhales the moisture-laden air, which is tinged with electricity. There is a throaty rumble from faraway thunder, and bolts of heat-lightning flicker on the horizon.

Walking toward the hanger where his Jeep is parked, he peeks through the doors at the high-winged PBY Catalina. He spots someone's feet positioned on a tall ladder under the port engine, and veers away from his Jeep to step inside. Recognizing the mechanic's canvas high-top sneakers, Flynn stops at the base of the ladder and calls up. "Hey, Wing Nut. Why are you working on her? I thought she was grounded?"

The mechanic sets a tool in the top tray of the stepladder and peers down at Flynn. "The lady has some possible buyers coming in next week to take a look at her." Knowing how Flynn feels about the vintage airplane, he is reluctant to say more, but he grabs another tool and continues. "She told me to get this old water-bird in tip-top shape."

Flynn shakes his head and grunts, "Dammit..."

"Sorry, Flynn..."

Clenching his fists and needing something to punch, the frustrated pilot looks around. With lips curled into an angry scowl, his harsh words come out as mumbled gibberish.

91

Wing Nut, looking down from the ladder, watches Flynn's animated shit-fit. "Everything okay, Buddy?"

Calming himself, Flynn finally heaves a resigned sigh. "Yeah, things are fine... I'm just having one of those days where the world seems stacked against me."

Wing Nut looks down at Flynn from the ladder and offers a consoling wink. "This sweet old bird will need to go on a test flight tomorrow if you happen to be around about five in the morning. Just be sure to show up before you-know-who arrives to start her day."

Reaching up, Flynn runs his hand along the metal belly of the flying boat and gives it an affectionate pat. "Thanks pal. I'll be here before first light, ready with my flying shoes on."

Wing Nut watches, as the pilot gives one last, lingering gaze at the seaplane before stepping away to his Jeep. "See ya tomorrow." The pilot lifts a hand skyward and gives a wave, as he climbs into his vehicle and starts the engine. The mud-spattered Jeep slowly backs up, turns and drives away.

~*~

A Jeep is parked outside the log cabin homestead. Above, flashes of lightning pop through menacing clouds. Flynn stands below the eaves of the covered front porch and looks out over the valley. He has an antique, lever-action Winchester rifle in his hands. On the porch rail sits a box of ammunition. He thumbs the box open and grabs several rounds.

After loading a dozen cartridges into the rifle's side-gate, Flynn cocks the lever and brings the walnut stock up under his chin and against his shoulder. He lines up the iron sights of the rifle toward a wooden farm wagon that sits out in the middle of a pasture. The old, abandoned wagon, surrounded by tall grass, sits canted on three broken-spoked wheels. Letting his aim linger and his thoughts wander,

Fire Angels

Flynn glances at his Jeep, thinking on the defining image of the dilapidated wagon set against the modern conveyance. Life's irony does not escape him, as he squeezes the trigger.

The sharp report of the gunshot is followed promptly by a splinter of wood flying off the top corner of the wagon's bed. He lowers the rifle and cocks the lever again to eject the empty brass shell casing. Flynn peers down at the spent cartridge as a wisp of black-powder smoke curls up from the metal casing. He lets out a long exhale and looks to the broken-down target. In a swift, fluid motion, he raises the rifle to his shoulder, squeezes off a shot, quickly cocks the lever and shoots again. With each rifle shot, splinters of broken wood fly off from the rotted wagon.

Finally, the rifle clicks empty, and Flynn looks down at the spent brass cartridge casings scattered all around his feet. He takes a deep breath before grabbing another handful of rounds from the box and pressing them into the loading gate. A flash of lightning flickers in the distance, followed shortly by a loud clap of thunder that rolls across the valley floor. Flynn looks to the gloomy sky and murmurs to himself. "There's a heck of a storm a' brewin'." Thumbing the last cartridge into the rifle magazine, he levers the action, raises the gun to his shoulder and fires.

~*~

It is completely dark inside the log cabin, except for a light from a kitchen appliance and the radio alarm clock glowing on the nightstand. The digital clock reads 3:14 a.m., and Flynn rolls over to adjust his blankets. A pulsing ring from the telephone at his bedside startles him awake, and he reaches over to take the cordless receiver from the base.

"Hello...?"

The familiar voice on the other end of the phone line sounds just as groggy. "Hey there, Flynn..." Chuck coughs to clear his throat and then croaks, "We just got a call, notifying us that there have been several lighting strikes in the area. There aren't any contracts on the fires yet, but they're nearby, so we were asked to be on call with a two hour standby." Flynn rubs his eyes and glances to the time on the clock. "Okay, Chuck… Thanks for the call."

He clicks off the cordless handset and, with a thud, sets it back down on the nightstand. Outside, the dark sky is brightened occasionally by remarkable flashes of lightning. Still lying in bed, Flynn watches nature's light show and waits for the rumbling cracks of thunder to follow. Closing his eyes, he drifts off again.

Chapter 22

At the Fire Angels headquarters, sheets of torrential rain are pouring down. Headlights piercing the darkness, splashing through deep puddles, Flynn's Jeep comes up the driveway and parks at his usual spot. He jumps out, swings his door shut and is quickly drenched before ducking into the hangar.

The overhead lights inside the domed metal building brightly illuminate the massive size of the Catalina seaplane. On the other side of the hangar, starting the day with cups of coffee in hand, aircraft mechanics perform maintenance on the other aircraft. Flynn shakes off the dampness, as he looks to the head mechanic climbing out of the nose hatch of the Catalina. "Mornin', Wing Nut. How's she doing?"

The mechanic grins and closes the seaplane's hatch. "For this vintage bird, you couldn't ask for anything more." Suddenly, a bright flash of lightning is followed by a rolling rumble of thunder. The two turn to look at the dark morning sky and the heavy rain pouring outside the hangar doors. Flynn laughs, "A fine day for flying…"

The mechanic climbs down the ladder and continues the thought. "… If you're a seaplane."

"Yeah, she's built for it." Looking over the Catalina, Flynn fondly admires the sweeping curve of the boat-like hull. His gaze lingers on the water scoops set into the plane's belly. He touches his fingertips to the cool metal skin and feels a tingle of excitement that seems to happen every time he gets to fly the converted warplane. Passing by the amphibious landing gear under the wing, Flynn goes to his locker at the back corner of the hangar.

He kicks off his rain-splashed cowboy boots, pulls on a Nomex flight suit and takes out a set of lace-up work boots. Flynn grabs a chair and sits to tie the laces of his flight boots. As Wing Nut approaches, Flynn looks up and asks, "Did anyone have anything to say about me taking the Catalina out for a run?"

The mechanic grins. "A lesson I learned from you is that it's better to ask for forgiveness than permission."

Flynn finishes the lacing on his boots and chuckles. "Good motto, but doesn't always work out the best for me. Let's get this old bird out of here, before anyone important shows up to ask questions."

~*~

The Old Man's Cadillac rolls up the puddled lane to the air base, and he turns his attention to the lights coming from the airplane hangar. He stops in front of the office building and glances over to Flynn's Jeep parked in its usual spot. Stepping out of his car, the rain quickly wets his silver hair, making it shimmer in the beam of the overhead security light.

A mischievous twinkle appears in Frederick's eye, as he watches the nose of the Catalina begin to roll out through the line of rain that drips down over the open hangar doors. Pushing back his wet hair, he softly clicks his car door closed and ducks in through the double front doorway of the office. The Cadillac's headlights blink off, as, across the way, the vintage seaplane slowly emerges from its hangar and into the torrential downpour.

~*~

Fire Angels

Once outside the hangar, Flynn climbs into the hatch of the amphibious seaplane and makes his way up to the cockpit. Sliding into the chair at the controls, he looks out the window to the supervising mechanic standing in the pouring rain. After flipping some switches and waving a confirmation to Wing Nut, Flynn pulls on his seat harness. As the pilot performs the preflight procedure, there is a steady patter of splashing raindrops on the windows. Flynn looks to the aircraft checklist balanced on his knee. Satisfied, he smiles as he gazes around the familiar cockpit. "It's good to be flying with you again, old girl."

A slight, bumping shudder comes from underneath the nose of the aircraft, as the pushback tractor stops to turn and then continues to drive the seaplane away from the hangar. Flynn clicks on the auxiliary power and activates the wiper blades on the windshield. Splashes of water on the windows are pushed aside, as Flynn looks out to the waiting air field.

The seaplane finally slowly rolls to a stop, and Flynn leans forward to see the pusher vehicle unhook and drive back to the shelter of the hangar. He gives the rain-slicked driver a wave and then faces forward. The exterior floodlights of the domed metal buildings glisten off the wet aircraft as Flynn makes an adjustment to the controls and goes through the procedure to start the engines. "Alright now, baby-girl… It's a little bit wet out here this morning, but that's what you were made for. Let's go for a ride." Overhead, the big radial engines fire up and the three blade propellers start to rotate and then spin faster.

Sitting high on the tricycle landing gear, the high-winged seaplane slowly rolls forward, through the sheets of blowing rain, toward the puddled runway. As the Catalina lines up in preparation for takeoff, the rain momentarily eases, and the seaplane can be seen clearly at the end of the air strip.

The spinning propellers appear to rotate backwards, as the engines throttle up and belch exhaust. The aircraft yearns to leap into the sky, but the brakes on the wheels hold it back.

In the upstairs office, a desktop light clicks on and then Frederick appears at the wide panel of observation windows. He listens to the revving of the dual engines, as the Catalina readies for take-off. Clutching both hands behind his back, he eagerly watches the seaplane release the wheel brakes and then lunge forward down the strip. Offering a waving salute, the Old Man observes the aircraft roaring down the runway to leap into the early morning sky.

Chapter 23

Beads of rainwater stream to the edges of the windshield, as Flynn climbs the aircraft to a higher altitude. He looks out over the expanse of forested terrain below, and then to the grey morning sky and its lingering twists of dark rainclouds. An occasional flash of lightning illuminates the clouds with an ominous appearance.

The radio headset crackles to life and Flynn moves his hand to adjust the microphone along his jaw to under his lip. The comforting tone of a familiar voice puts a wide grin on Flynn's face. "It's the Old Man here… We don't even have to guess who took off in our Catalina."

"And a good morning to you!"

"You do plan on bringing it back, don't you?"

Flynn gazes at the mountain scenery below and laughs. "Just out for a quick spin after some routine maintenance." The radio crackles with loud static for a moment and then returns. "Yeah… Routine, my ass. While you're up there joy-riding, you can scout out some lightning strikes to the northwest."

Flynn veers the airplane to the north. "Copy that."

As an orange ray of sunshine breaks through the clouds on the horizon, Flynn squints and puts on his pilot sunglasses. He stares ahead to the narrow beam of sunlight framed by the dark clouds and grins. "It's a beautiful day for flying."

The glistening body of the PBY Catalina banks harder and tips its wings further north, as more rays of sunshine break through the storm clouds.

~*~

Seated at the big desk in the Fire Angels headquarters, Frederick scans his eyes over several stacks of papers before turning to look through the bay of windows toward the landing field. He hears a set of women's heels coming up the stairway and gets a feeling of dread in the pit of his stomach. Camille makes her way up the stairs, turns the corner and offers a friendly nod to him as she puts down her briefcase. He watches her take a seat and get settled-in with some paperwork. As she sits back in her chair, he lifts a paper from the pile and spins it across the desktop. "Ms. Vanderhaus, where are we on that PBY Catalina?"

She looks over at him curiously, hesitates and replies, "I have some interested buyers coming by to look at it."

"Who?"

"Two of them are air parks and one is private."

"Museums?"

"Yes."

"When?"

"Next week."

He turns to look out the window at the remaining storm clouds and retorts, "Give them a call back and tell them not to bother. It's not for sale anymore."

Confused, Camille stares at him. "And why is that?"

"It is a good, mid-size tanker... And we need it."

She shakes her head with frustration, as they have already had this exact same conversation. "It is worth a lot more to these collectors than what we get from sending it out. That money will offset the cost of the C-130s coming in."

Fire Angels

Continuing to stare out the window, Frederick speaks low and direct. "Cancel them too." Squirming in her seat, Camille looks around the vacant office, failing to find anything that has changed since she was there the day prior. Trying to stifle her irritation, she asks, "What's going on? What about this situation is different since we last spoke?"

"Nothing... I've had a change of heart."

Camille sits up straighter in her chair and snarls at him. "I don't care if you've had a pleasant change of underwear... We have a written agreement to acquire and appraise this outfit of yours, and, if you don't fulfill your monetary obligations to the contract, we can take the whole thing away from you and just scrap it all!"

Understanding her adverse reaction, he studies her. "Yes, Ms. Vanderhaus, I know what the agreement says."

"Then what the hell is wrong with you? If you get another year like last year on the books, or like the year before, you're all done here." She searches the room again for anyone who might have influenced this recent turn of events. "It will be the end for you and every one of these hot-shots."

The Old Man presents her with a long stare before turning to gaze out the bay of windows again. "I know..."

Rising from her chair, Camille steps over to stand before Frederick's cluttered desk. "I'm *trying* to help you here. Some of the small things we've already completed are good, but they're a drop in the bucket if we don't get the short term contracts that are up for grabs during the fire season."

Still watching out the windows, he speaks over his shoulder to the perturbed businesswoman looming behind. "The big tankers can only operate out of the larger airfields. The heart and soul of my crew is here. If we dice 'em up and spread 'em all over, then what will we have?"

"You might still have a business to operate."

He nods understandingly and takes a deep breath. "There are a lot of ways to die in life... And with business, some of them are quick and some slow."

Putting her hands to her hips, she shakes her head. "The aerial fire-bombing business has changed with the times, and you've been dying a slow death for the last few years."

"At least it has been in a lifestyle I can still enjoy."

She shakes her head, glances around the empty office and then looks out the windows to the early morning sky, trying to comprehend what he might possibly be staring at. "Do you understand that if you don't have every plane you've got up in the air for most of the season, you're done for?"

"Yes... I understand."

Camille places her hands on his desk and firmly states, "The company I work for is not going to offer another chance. In a second, they will sell this whole operation off to the scrap yard and land developers without thinking twice about it."

Frederick continues to longingly stare out the window, clenching his jaw tight to hold his strong emotions at bay. "Yes... I get the picture."

Camille shakes her head and heaves a troubled sigh. "You know, I didn't have to come to help save this outfit." Standing straight, she crosses her arms. "There are jobs that I would much rather have taken."

Frederick turns to look directly at the assertive woman. "And why was it you came here, exactly? I was a bit surprised, myself, when they informed me that they were sending their top person to handle things." He stares at her questioningly. "Your company handles acquisitions of much larger operations than this small potato."

She hesitates with her answer, and a twinkle of recognition shimmers in the Old Man's eyes. Finally, she responds, "Yes, well... I have my reasons."

Fire Angels

He nods sympathetically. "I have my own reasons, too. I really think we can make this work better without slicing and dicing the crew and airplanes we already have."

They study each other for a moment, until they finally come to a silent understanding. Camille turns, paces the length of his desk twice before stopping and facing him again. Despite being put off, she finally nods her agreement. "Fine, the Catalina can stay in the fleet, but we still need to bring in the big tankers to qualify for the larger contracts."

He thinks a while, turns back to the window and sighs. "Okay, you can still bring in the bigger tankers. We'll fly them for this season and, if we can fulfill our end of the partnership agreement, we'll keep this outfit intact."

After scanning the clutter-filled office once again, Camille turns back to face Frederick, lamenting, "Yes, that's what the contractual agreement states, but I don't see how you can do it without trimming the crew and selling off the unnecessary equipment."

The skies start to brighten, as more beams of light break through the storm clouds. Frederick stands from his chair and, followed by Camille, steps to the window. They both notice the shining rays of morning sun reflect off the puddle-strewn runway, before he glances at her and snorts his rebuttal, "These boys may operate a bit on the fringes, but they're all damn good flyers and know how to perform their jobs well when it comes to putting out wildfires."

Head tilted, arms crossed over her chest, Camille states, "Yes… Well, they better be as good as you say if you hope to make it through this season with money on the books." Camille's eyes flit to the older man, and she adds, sincerely, "For *everyone's* sake, I hope you're right…"

Standing up straighter, staring out to the airfield as the crew starts to arrive and another day begins, Frederick replies,

Eric H. Heisner

"If we don't make it, we'll just have to go out on our own terms, doing what we do best."

Chapter 25

Already dressed in his flight suit, Floyd "the Fish" holds a small paperback novel in his hand. He slaps it on the table when he sees Flynn approach from the open hangar doors. "Hot-damn, you marvelous thing... You snuck out with the flying boat! Just how many fires did you spot up there?"

"Over a dozen."

Fish whistles. "Hell of a light show last night."

From the wide doorway, Kansas Sam steps into the hangar and makes his way to the back corner. He sees Floyd all suited up, and then watches Flynn go to his gear locker. "The reports are in that they have ground-crews assigned and are looking to contract us for the rougher terrain stuff."

Flynn nods. "If they don't get some control of it soon, the whole state of Idaho will be cooked like a baked potato."

A metal locker door creaks open and Kansas Sam tosses his big duffle bag inside, replying, "They've called everyone in, and we're supposed to have a briefing in half an hour."

Fish smiles his oddball grin and glances at Flynn. "Hopefully it's not just another one of those scolding sessions about how *loosey-goosey*, here..." Fish hooks a thumb aside. "...was doing something he was not supposed to be doing."

They both look directly at Flynn, who innocently smiles. "Who, *me*? What have *I* done lately?"

Both of the fire-pilots immediately look out the open hangar doors to the big PBY Catalina tanker aircraft outside. Kansas Sam takes off his sunshades and cleans them on the bottom of his T-shirt. "From what I overheard this morning, you might have saved the Catalina from its retirement."

Perplexed, Flynn asks, "How's that?"

"When the Old Man saw her flying again, he got a good dose of that old-time feeling and put his foot down with the skirt about not selling her."

Chip strolls into the hangar and grumbles at them. "Don't lift up your dresses to congratulate each other just yet. If we don't fulfill that main contract with the corporate suits, everything goes to the chopping block in one fell swoop."

Every pilot turns to look at the mustached flyer, and Fish pipes in. "The season is just starting up."

"Yep, and we got a long ways to go."

Sam puts his sunshades on and mutters in agreement. "The burn season seems to get longer every year."

Ambling toward them, Chip swipes his finger under his lip to sweep the ends of his moustache aside and nods his head in reply. "And, if we don't watch our tail, keep our noses clean and do our jobs to the best of our ability, it will be our last hurrah." Chip drops his flight duffle on an empty chair, rakes his fingers through his greying hair and looks to each of the aviators. He tilts his head in the direction of the office. "Let's go find out what we're all in for with this one."

~*~

On the ground floor of the Fire Angels main building, the recreation room is packed wall to wall with pilots and ground-crew members. Leading the assembly, the Old Man has a bit of his spirit back and lacks the hang-dog look that he had at the prior group meeting. Shoulders pulled back, Frederick stands before the crowd. All eyes are on him as he calls out, "Listen up, boys...!" Glancing over at Camille next to the empty bar, he lowers his voice. "No disrespect to the ladies, of course." Continuing his address to the fire-fighters, he loudly expresses, "We have reports coming in that we have over a dozen surface burns with potential for some real damage to local homes. Ground-crews are trying to get to most of them, but a few are tucked in some rough terrain. They're calling in smoke jumpers now, and our job will be to assist and protect them, so they can do their work safely."

The years of mileage on Frederick's features melt away, as he fulfills his true calling as a leader of men. He lets his gaze travel around the room, recognizing and acknowledging each of his longtime employees, and then resumes his speech. "I know it's been a rough couple of weeks... Hell, it's been a rough couple of years!" After a chuckle of amusement travels through the room, he continues. "Now, we're gonna leave that behind us and do what we're trained to do: fly it low, fly it slow, and get in there to put out some damned wildfires!" Frederick turns to Camille and gives her an encouraging nod. "Miss Vanderhaus, here, has put together the list of crews for the initial fire suppression runs. She has carefully assessed key talents along with the pairing of an aircraft. Let her do her job, so you can do yours."

The chatter in the room dies down, as Camille steps forward with her clipboard. She glances down at her notes before looking around at the attentive crew of fire-fighters. "At this time, our main focus is to support the crews that have been deployed on the ground. We have been notified of several primary surface burns, and we will serve as aerial support and fire suppression to keep a line of defense for the most populated areas."

There is a charge of excitement in the air, as they anticipate the work at hand. Camille noticeably relaxes, as she looks confidently at the group of men who are more than capable at doing their jobs. Her eyes stop at Flynn, lingering a moment before she glances down at her clipboard again.

"We're going to start with some of the small aircraft to get in the tight spots and nip these surface burns in the bud." She clicks her pen, clears her throat and turns to Wing Nut. "Support crews, you already have your orders and know what needs to be done." Her gaze travels across the room until it falls upon Woody Pyle, and she quickly looks away. "The rest of you, join me upstairs. We'll have a look at the maps of the drop sites and assign tanker aircraft."

At the back of the room, Woody folds his arms on his chest, while his colleagues gradually make their way upstairs. The room slowly clears out, as mechanics and ground-crew depart through the double front doors. He listens to the sound of feet shuffling up the wooden stair treads as the pilots proceed to the office. Left dejected and alone, Woody shakes his head and slumps into a chair near the back wall.

Chapter 26

Fire-bombing aircrafts roll out from every hangar and line up on the taxiway, waiting for their turn to take off. The entire air base is consumed with bustling activity backed by the rumble and roar of the planes lifting off. After hooking up the water drop bucket, Floyd and Kansas Sam climb inside the chopper. The helicopter's engine begins to whine, and the rotators slowly turn the long, floppy blades. The spinning rotor warms up, sending a heavy draft downward against the grass.

Next in line on the airstrip, Chip revs the engines of the recently-repaired P-2 Neptune and prepares for takeoff. Seated at the controls, Chip listens to the radio chatter and smiles when he hears a call come in for him. "Hey there, Chip! Ya better practice your failed-engine flying with that clipped-wing bird."

"Thanks, Flynn..." Chip adjusts his headset and finishes his preflight checklist. "I won't have a passenger to critique my every move, and you probably chased out all the squirrels for me."

The radio signal is momentarily overcome with static, until Flynn's voice comes back, loud and clear. "Copy that... See you in the air, Buddy."

~*~

Engines rev, and the blast of air from propellers blows loose debris across the ground. Next to takeoff, the P-2 Neptune releases its breaks and lunges down the runway. Through the front windshield, the mustached pilot salutes the ground-crew as he zooms past. The forward wheel on the tricycle landing gear rises from the ground and the aircraft lifts into the sky.

Jockeying into position to depart next, Chuck, in the Fire Boss aircraft, faces its amphibious pontoons out toward the takeoff strip. The single, high-powered engine at the nose of the aircraft buzzes like an angry hive of bees. Throttled up, it quickly pulls the small seaplane down a short stretch of runway before lifting off. Gaining altitude, Chuck banks northwest, following after Chip in the Neptune.

Bringing-up the rear, Flynn sits in the cockpit of the twin engine, tail-dragger PV-2 Harpoon. The profile of the aircraft distinctly defines it as a World War II surplus model. The twin-finned tail section gives it a unique appearance, as it sits at the end of the runway preparing for take-off.

Flynn watches departing aircraft fade to the horizon and then looks over as Floyd and Sam lift off in the helicopter. With the bucket dangling below, the chopper climbs higher before pitching its nose down and following after the others. Temporarily easing up on one of the aircraft's wheel brakes, Flynn turns the high-tilted nose of the Harpoon to line up with the pink-hued runway. The engines rev one more time, and then Flynn releases both brakes.

Leaning forward, Flynn peers over the elevated nose of the aircraft as it zooms down the airfield. As the tail section slowly rises, he sits up straight with a clearer view out ahead. The aircraft levels and he pushes back in the seat, easing the yoke to his lap until the speeding airplane lifts off the strip.

Fire Angels

Gaining altitude, the PV-2 Harpoon gradually banks to the heading of the other departed airplanes.

~*~

Fire Angels planes and a single helicopter fly in a loose formation toward the distant and ever-increasing clouds of smoke. The single engine Fire-Boss floatplane flies in the lead, with Chip and Flynn flying nearby on opposite flanks. Chuck's voice breaks through the radio static. "Okay, fellas... We got a few of 'em to take care of, but they ain't much yet. Our job is to keep 'em from spreading out, so those boys on the ground can snuff 'em."

The small formation gradually approaches the columns of smoke rising from the forest floor. Leading the charge, Chuck directs their attack. "Flynn, you start by taking out number three, on the right, and Chip... Follow me through to the left on number eight. Let's try to drop the load just ahead of that burn, and it might smolder itself out."

Flynn pipes in. "Copy that, Fire Boss."

There is a brief stretch of radio static, and Chip confirms the plan of attack. "Copy... I'm on your six and following your lead, Fire Boss." The three airplanes break formation, and Chuck's voice comes on the radio again. "Kansas... You and Fish work that Bambi bucket on number eleven fire near the reservoir."

The radio crackles until the chopper pilot responds, "You betcha, Fire-Boss... We are on it like hot on sauce!" Whirling away, the helicopter pivots and flies toward a tree-bordered reservoir, in the valley below.

~*~

Each of the planes dives down to a few hundred feet over the trees to drop their payload to the leading edges of their targeted fires. The mixture of fire-retardant and water washes over the landscape and blankets the wooded area with a fine, rosy mist. On the ground, Hotshot crews move along the front lines of the fire, clearing away groundcover that could fuel the burn.

Near the reservoir, the helicopter with its Bambi bucket hovers over a flare-up farther away from the other fires. Kansas Sam and Floyd drop a load of water and then swing back to fill-up again. Circling high above the action, Chuck directs everyone to the next targeted drops.

Chapter 27

In the cockpit of the PV-2 Harpoon, Flynn shows signs of exhaustion after having completed his sixth run of the day. Off his left wing, he looks out the window toward Chip in the Neptune and repositions the headset microphone at his chin. "Hey Chip, this one should be the last run of the day."

"Yep... We'll be losing light in another hour."

Tipping his wings and peering down to the smoldering terrain below, he sees clusters of ground-crew still at work. Flynn levels his wings and glances toward Chip's aircraft. "Sure glad we're working up here. It looks like they'll be on coyote-tactics for a few days to keep that smolder contained."

The Neptune banks toward the drop sight, and Chip replies. "I'd rather be *over* it than *in* it any day."

As the pair of water-bombing aircraft approach the last targeted drop-site of the afternoon, Chuck circles high above the rising smoke in the single engine Fire-Boss pontoon plane. His voice crackles in on the radio, interrupting their banter. "Nice of you fellas to join me for one last dump before dusk."

Flynn pipes in. "Where do you want it, pal?"

"Just follow me..."

The three airplanes line up in formation and make their way toward the location of another rising column of smoke. Constantly scanning around the area, Flynn stays focused on the blazing treetops and the airplanes flying alongside him.

He looks at Chuck in the single-engine plane, slightly ahead, and listens as the familiar voice breaks through on the radio. "We'll all drop our payload on this one and head for home." The radio crackles, and Chuck continues. "Try to overshoot my line, and we'll have it cut off from the fresh timber."

The airplanes fall in line and prepare to dump their loads on the wildfire below. First to aim his nose downward, Chuck steers his aircraft toward the treetops and releases his drop tank just short of the fire line. Following in the Harpoon, Flynn dives down, coming in just above the flaming treetops. His plane, roaring over the fire licking up from the timber, starts to release its retardant and water mix just beyond the hissing path of the previous drop. Seconds later, the tanks are emptied and, with a roar of engines, he pulls up to pass through a zero-visibility column of smoke.

Dripping with sweat, Flynn flies the airplane blindly through the increasing turbulence and grayish-orange haze. The heat in the cabin climbs to an uncomfortable level, as Flynn continues to pull upward through the polluted sky. Finally, visibility increases, as he breaks through the cloud and banks away from the thick column of rising smoke. Spotting Chuck circling above, Flynn turns his aircraft on a heading toward home base.

Out his left-side window, Flynn watches Chip dive in toward the drop zone and fly low over the blazing treetops. The Neptune cruises through the smoky haze. Finally, the water-tank hatch opens up, and the crimson mixture is expelled from the belly of the aircraft to spread over the forest.

Successfully completing the drop, Chip charges through an updraft of colored flames, pulling his airplane up. The Neptune water-bomber momentarily vanishes from sight. Then, with smoke clinging to its tail section, it roars out the other side of the haze.

Fire Angels

Gaining altitude while circling his aircraft, Flynn sees Chip fly out the other side of the turbulent column of smoke. He heaves a sigh of relief and touches the brim of his cap. Holding the headset mic closer to his mouth, he comments, "Nice drop, Chipper. Let's head for home..."

As the last words escape his mouth, a sudden flash of light catches Flynn's eye, and he sees one of the Neptune's radial engines instantly engulfed in flames. Flynn banks his aircraft toward the compromised water-bomber, but, before he can utter another word, the whole pair of engines explodes. The blast separates the wing from the fuselage, the airplane turns over, and then it drops.

The explosion mirrors in Flynn's sunglasses as he watches the aircraft suddenly tumble into a spinning dive toward the trees below. In shock, Flynn watches the fiery destruction of his friend's plane. *"Chip...!"* Overtaken with grief, Flynn circles his aircraft over the flaming wreckage. Eventually, he swallows a rising lump in his throat and croaks a few words into his radio mic. "Harpoon two-twenty to fire base... We have an aircraft down north-east of drop-site nine."

Radio static and the drone of the airplane's engines echo empty through Flynn's mind, as he struggles to accept and wake from this nightmare. The Harpoon continues to circle, as the radio crackles and the controller answers back. "Affirmative... What is the status of the pilot?"

Flynn swallows hard, as he looks to the burning wreck below. Still not able to believe his eyes, he circles his airplane again and finally responds... "I don't think Chip made it."

~*~

On the fumes of a near-empty fuel tank, Flynn flies back to the Fire Angels air base. In the last of the evening light, he brings the aircraft in for a gentle, unhurried landing.

Regaining control before tears well up, Flynn glances over his shoulder. "I don't really feel like entertaining today."

"It wasn't your fault."

Flynn nods and turns around to face her. "I know... Blaming myself wouldn't make a difference, anyhow."

Anxious, Camille wants to say something, but doesn't. Flynn stares at her, and the awkward silence makes it feel a lot like old times. He momentarily puts aside his defensive demeanor and asks her, "Did you happen to come out here for a particular reason?"

As she continues to quietly rock in the chair, he gets impatient. "Camille, I'm having a bad day, so if you don't have anything to say, I'll just excuse myself."

Her response to his aggravation is a simple smile. Appreciating the comforting solitude, she looks past him to the peaceful, mountain valley. As wind blows through the distant trees, she finally comments, "This is a nice place to be."

He nods and shifts his positon on the porch railing. "Yeah, it's quiet enough. I like it alright."

"Is this where you want to end up?"

"You mean when I stop flying or when I'm buried?"

Camille shrugs, unsure if there is a difference for him. She looks around the porch for a moment and then replies, "You know, I always figured you'd stop flying someday and get your feet on the ground..."

"I'd rather go out like Chip did."

Her drifting gaze travels back to him and, in her eyes, a glimmer of heartfelt emotion breaks through her hardened exterior. "That is a very lonely way to go."

In an attempt to lighten the somber mood, he jokes. "I'd rather not take anyone else along with me when I go." Unamused, she rolls her eyes and gazes back out to the mountains. "Do you ever think about us anymore?"

Fire Angels

There is a lengthy pause as he stares at her. She avoids his gaze by keeping her attention on the faraway tree line. Flynn clicks his teeth together, clenches his jaw, and then softly mutters, "I never stopped thinking about you."

She gulps, as her eyes flit to him. "Really?"

"Yeah. And, lately, a whole lot more than before..." Her uncertain gaze locks with his. Flynn stands upright and takes a step toward her. He bends down and places both hands on the arms of the rocking chair. Holding the chair firm, he positions his face directly before hers. She looks at him intently, as he quietly whispers, "If I wasn't who I am, and you weren't such a..."

"Oh, shut up already..." She reaches her hands up, placing them on each side of Flynn's face to pull it toward her. Their lips gradually move closer until they feel a familiar touch. They kiss, expressing the pent-up passion that has been building through the weeks since her arrival at the air base. While still locked in their kiss, Flynn stands her up from the porch rocker, reaches his arm around her and embraces her tightly. Between groping kisses, Camille utters, "Aren't you going to..." Flynn pulls himself back to look at her as she finishes her sentence. "... offer a lady a drink?"

Flynn smiles before squeezing her tight again and kissing her deeply, as he kicks out a booted foot to open the front door of the cabin. "Would you like to come in?"

Camille clutches Flynn's torso while spinning him around to slam him up against the door frame. Both breathing heavily, she remarks, "I don't know... Do you think it would be proper?"

Keeping a tight grasp on her backside, Flynn gazes into her upturned eyes. "This is how I treat all my wives."

"Is there a long list?"

"Long enough... You're the only one on it."

She shrugs and defiantly turns a cheek toward him. "Maybe if you weren't such a little kid..." She turns to look directly at him.

He stares sincerely into her eyes and states, "Maybe if you weren't such a b..."

Camille quickly presses her lips to his, and she pulls him in through the cabin doorway. The door swings freely on its hinges, as furniture is bumped and a lamp crashes to the floor. Suddenly, a mountain breeze sweeps across the porch. The rocking chairs tilt back and, with a solid *bang*, the cabin's front door sucks closed. A bed frame creaks, followed by Camille's nearly breathless voice. "Oh Flynn, I missed you..."

~*~

Strong gusts of wind blow ash across the charred remains of the forest floor. Several glowing embers flare-up and drift toward fresh tinder and years-worth of amassed organic fuel. Over the mountain ridge, in a clearing not far from the recent fires, a Hotshot crew surrounded by their tools and protective gear, prepares to bed down for the night.

Chapter 29

The inside of Flynn's rustic, one room cabin is illuminated by the amber glow of a single lamp. Flynn and Camille lie next to each other on the bed. Flipping back the tousled covers, Flynn sits up and swings his legs over the side. Scratching his chest, he is about to stand when a female voice, muffled through the pillow, murmurs. "Where are you going?"

He turns, looking at the woman in his bed, and smirks. "Well, I can't sneak out, since this is my place."

Unamused, she grunts, "Next time we do this at mine, and you can leave anytime you'd like."

Flynn slides off the bed and makes his way across the room to the refrigerator. He pulls the handle and the light of the appliance's bright interior shines out into the cabin as he reaches in to grab a beer. Glancing behind to the bed, he notices that she has the covers pulled over her head to block the blinding light. "You need anything?"

"I'll just have a sip of yours... Shut that door, please." Flynn frowns and pulls another can of beer from the fridge. He walks to the bed, while cracking open one of the cans and hands it to her. She takes the cold beer and sits up, holding the covers under her arms. Camille crinkles her brow, giving Flynn an odd look. "I said I only wanted a sip."

"Well, I wanted a whole one."

"Would just a sip from yours really kill you?"

Flynn cracks his beer can open and takes a long swig. "Let's say they're both mine, and you can have as many sips as you like from that one without pissing me off."

With the beer can in hand, Camille holds the covers tightly against her chest, as she scoots herself up against the headboard. "What if I don't want all of this?"

Flynn slips back into the bed next to Camille and pulls up the covers. "I'll drink it when you're done."

"What if it gets warm?"

"If I don't want it, I'll throw it away."

Irritated, Camille takes a short sip and leers at him. "Why are you always so damned stubborn?"

He looks beside at her and seems genuinely surprised at her sudden agitation. "Why is there even a problem?"

"Because you won't even share!"

He takes another gulp from his can of beer and grunts. "I did share... And I even got out of bed to get it for you."

"You were getting yourself one anyway."

"Yeah, and I got one for you too."

Camille purses her lips upset. "That's *not* the point..."

Scooting down to lean back on the headboard, Flynn shakes his head, sighing. "*Gratitude* is *your* problem..."

"*What*...?"

"You aren't even grateful that I gifted you a whole beer to yourself."

She takes another little sip and rolls her eyes at him. "Some gift! I told you I didn't want a *whole* beer."

Staring ahead, he comments. "That's two so far..."

"Two what?"

Smiling at her, he scrunches deeper under the covers, getting comfortable. "Sips you've taken..."

Her buttons pushed, she glares at him and then slams the beer can on the bedside table. "I don't even *want* it now!"

128

Fire Angels

He takes a drink from his own and peers over at her. "Pass it over here, then... *I'll* drink it."

Very frustrated, Camille continues to glare at Flynn. "Do you ever wonder why we didn't work out?"

"Not at the moment..."

She turns sideways in the bed to face him and jabs a pointed finger in his direction. "*You* are the reason!"

Situated just right with his head tilted against the headboard, Flynn takes another swallow from his beer and shrugs. "I'm half of it at least."

Not wanting to engage with him anymore, she crosses her arms, turns and stares across the room. They sit in silence, until she eventually grabs the beer from the side table and takes another sip. Glancing slyly at him, she mutters, "If you mention the sip count out loud, I'll smack you."

"I know."

She gives a soft growl, as she clutches the cold can of beer. As quickly as her temper flared, Camille is calm again. After looking around the small cabin, she looks over at Flynn who seems nearly asleep. "Did you ever want kids?"

Narrowly opening his eyes, he nods and grins at her. "Yeah, I always wanted bunches of 'em."

"Well, I can't do bunches."

With a sidelong look, he asks, "Why not?"

Camille takes another swallow and smiles demurely. "I'm almost forty years old."

"So?"

Taking a deep breath, she huffs. "You should be one to know how cruel Mother Nature can be." He continues to look at her endearingly, so she groans and explains to him further. "The thing is, by the time you're ready to have kids and can afford them, it's usually too late."

Flynn raises an eyebrow and smirks. "Not for me."

Camille gives him a cold stare. "You are *such* a jerk." Mockingly, she adds, "You *deserve* to be that old, grandpa-looking dad in his eighties when his kids graduate school."

Flynn sits and thinks, taking a long pause. As he swishes his can of beer, he can't help but smile and chuckle. "How young is the *mother* of those kids?"

Camille takes another drink from her beer and groans. "All I know is that she better be *very* young and *really dumb* to put up with you and your offspring."

"*Pretty* would be nice to have on that checklist, too..."

"Looks can fade..."

Flynn shrugs, takes a sip, and jiggles the remainder of the beer in the nearly-empty can. "Ahhh, I'll be really old and too blind by then to notice."

She rolls her eyes and takes another sip from her beer, while Flynn tips his can back to finish his. He looks at her in the bed beside him and smiles, knowingly. "That was a lot of sips."

She looks at the aluminum can in her hand and considers dumping it on him. "Are you still counting?"

"I lost count after five or six."

"Yeah, then you would have had to use both hands."

Flynn looks at his beer in hand and then smiles at her. "Who says I don't have my priorities straight?"

They lie next to each other in comfortable silence while they listen to the wind outside the cabin howl through the trees. A strong gust sends leaves skittering across the corrugated tin roof. Camille takes another sip, puts her drink aside and says, softly, "I'm tired... Mind if I sleep here?"

Flynn pats her bare bottom under the covers, smiles jauntily and replies, "Be my guest. The couch is available."

She swats his hand away. "*You* go sleep on the couch..." Rolling away from him onto her shoulder, she pulls the covers up, tucks them around her neck and snuggles into the pillow. He crunches his empty beer can and studies the female form tucked under the blankets. Before she has a chance to fall asleep, he taps her playfully on her curved hip. "You finished with that?"

"What?"

"My beer… That you were only having a sip from…" Reaching out from the covers, Camille grabs the nearly-full can and holds it out behind her without turning toward him. Graciously, Flynn takes it, swishes the remainder and smiles. "Good-night, Sweetie."

She mumbles quietly, as she attempts to fall asleep. "Shut off the light, fly-boy." Flynn sits up in bed, finishes-off the beer and sets the empty can aside on the bedside table. Satisfied, he looks around the dimly-lit room before scooching down into the covers. Camille opens her eyes a bit and turns her head toward him. "What about the lamp?"

He reaches out of the covers, gives two sharp claps of his hands and, on command, the light blinks off. In the dark, moonlit cabin, Camille's voice penetrates from the blackness. "Oh, my gosh… You are *such* a dork."

Flynn laughs, turns over on his side, and then playfully grabs at her under the bedsheets. "Thanks for coming over." She tries to ignore his groping hands and hides a demure grin. "I didn't figure there was going to be a written invite."

Flynn sits up and takes a long look at her. "Camille, you've always got an invite." He notices that she doesn't turn her head to acknowledge, and he lies back down. About to say something else, he instead, takes a breath and decides to keep it to himself.

The covers shift around as Flynn gets comfortable. Camille looks back at him in the blue-tinted light from the digital alarm clock. She stares at his dark form a minute and listens to him quickly drift off and slip into the heavy breathing of a soft snore. Amazed at how quickly he can fall asleep, she whispers, "Good night, Flynn."

Chapter 30

On the forested ridge above Flynn's cabin, powerful gusts of wind bend the treetops over, as the sky begins to brighten up with a new morning. The sun glows behind the mountain top, but it hasn't crested high enough shine on the valley below. The sleek, new Mercedes, out of place alongside the mud-spattered Jeep, is still parked in front of the cabin.

Several deer dart from the shelter of the timber and scamper across the wind-blown grasses carpeting the valley floor. Opposite the sunrise, on the far horizon, an ominous cloud of smoke gradually appears. The hazy firmament is accented by the orange glow of daylight.

~*~

A cellular phone ringing is quickly followed by the pulsing tone of Flynn's landline telephone. Half-asleep, he reaches across the bed and grabs the receiver from the cradle. Before he can even utter a word, Camille, with a blanket wrapped around her middle, is out of bed searching for her bulky, mobile telephone under a pile of her clothes.

Flynn answers first. "Hello?"

Camille ducks away and then answers her own call. "Hello, this is Camille…"

Still lying in bed, Flynn watches her slink away to the corner of the cabin for privacy, while he replies to the caller.

"Okay…Yeah… Be there in a few…" He tosses the covers aside, hops out of bed and pulls on a pair of crumpled pants.

It is only a moment before Camille clicks her cellular phone off, sets it down, and turns to look at him. She exclaims, "The fires have escalated!"

"Yeah… I just heard."

She comes back to the bed and fumbles with her pile of clothing while trying to keep the blanket wrapped to conceal her nakedness. "I have to go… I have to get to the air base."

Flynn looks outside, noticing the hinting light of early morning. Sitting at the edge of the bed, he scratches his head and watches her gather up her things. "What's the big hurry?" Looking past her to the hall leading to the bathroom, he grins. "Care for a shower?"

Camille looks at him, cracks a smile and dumps her stuff on the bed. "I have time for a quick one… *by myself…*"

Moving to an armoire, he shrugs as he opens it and pulls out a fresh towel for her. "Mind if I watch?"

"Yes, I *do* mind." She takes the towel from his hand, turns and lets the concealing blanket fall to the floor, as she saunters down the hallway. The bathroom door snaps closed behind her, followed by the clicking sound of a locking latch. Flynn takes a deep breath and sighs, as he bends down to pick up the empty beer cans from the night prior.

~*~

Flynn's Jeep pulls up to the Fire Angels headquarters and parks alongside the shiny, black Mercedes. He steps out, looks around the air base and then at the runway windsock. The orange, fabric tube stands perpendicular to the pole, drops down momentarily and then, catching another blast of wind, it snaps straight out to point in the other direction. Flynn turns his gaze upward to the storm clouds swirling above and lets out a soft groan. "Not a nice day for flying…"

Fire Angels

Stepping through the double doors to the meeting place below the main office, Flynn scans the crowded room and makes his way over to the group of pilots lining the bar. Bellying up, he nods to Kansas Sam, Chuck and then Woody. "Hey boys, there is a hell of a breeze blowing out there."

Chuck scratches the nape of his neck, as he looks over to reply to Flynn. "All air-drops are called off because of it, and the foot crews are struggling to battle the flare-ups."

Scanning the crowd in the room, Flynn notices a lot of new faces. Before he can ask who they are, Woody speaks. "They got the local Hotshot crews using the Fire Angel base as a jumping-off point to attack these fires. Flynn nods his understanding and turns back to the small group of pilots. "What's the current situation with the big C-130s we have coming in from the Forest Service?"

Woody pipes in. "They're on their way to the air base in Pocatello right now." The clamor in the room lowers some, as several of the Hotshot crewmen make their way outside. Flynn watches them go, leans back on the bar top and asks, "They got crews assigned to fly them yet?"

Woody responds, "We haven't heard."

At the bottom of the stairway leading up to the office, Floyd whistles loudly and waves the group of pilots over. "Hey, fellas! The Old Man wants to see us upstairs."

~*~

The lineup of fire-fighting pilots files up the stairs to the office and makes its way through a crowded room bustling with new faces. Nonstop phone calls are being answered, as reports of fire locations are charted on maps. Flynn looks across the room, briefly connecting his gaze with Camille's. He follows the group to the observation windows, where Frederick sits behind his desk. To make room on the desktop, the old man stands and pushes aside stacks of reports and tubes of rolled maps.

The founder of the air base looks to the familiar faces before him, and nods a sincere welcome. There seems to be a noticeable void in the group due to the absence of Chip. Frederick coughs to clear his throat and begins. "Hello, boys... It seems that, just overnight, we got a real mess on our hands. Those dry winds we've had blowing-in the last few days have turned almost all the controlled surface burns into firestorms." Gesturing to a map on the desk, he points at the northwest corner. "We have blow-ups around here, here and here..."

Slowly, he traces his finger along the mountainous ridge-line surrounding a lake. "These fires here have almost come together, and we're hoping they'll burn each other out." He looks up to assess his crew of pilots before he continues. "The strong winds and the fire's proximity to the shoreline make it too dangerous to use the lake for any water pickups. Maybe if these winds calm down a bit, we might be able to get the chopper in there with the bucket."

Gravely serious, the Old Man looks directly at the airmen assembled before him. "The wind gusts are currently too strong for our smaller aircraft to safely do low-level drops. There are C-130s from the forestry department coming in to Pocatello, and one of them needs experienced men to fly it." His gaze drops to the map on the desk, and then he looks out the bay of windows to the bustling ground-crew activity outside. "I'll need volunteers to head over there and fly it. They want to clear them for drops as soon as the winds are safe enough for the bigger tankers."

Flynn leans-in over the desktop and sneaks a glimpse toward Camille, who has drifted closer along the sidelines. While she appears to be doing form-filling on her clipboard, she listens intently. Her gaze drifts to the map spread out on the desk, and she pretends not to notice him watching her. Flynn raises his hand to volunteer. "I'm game to fly one of those big birds."

Floyd taps the table with his knuckles and grunts. "Well, I kinder like riding them big ol' ladies, so I'll go, too." At the back of the group Woody coughs to get their attention. "I'd like to go along as Flight Engineer."

Taking a deep breath, Frederick looks over at Camille who shakes her head. He grimaces, as he turns his attention back to Woody. "Sorry, pal. We've already talked about this."

The pilots all step aside and make room for Woody to move forward. He lets out a troubled sigh. "Excuse me, sir. With us being shorthanded, because of... well, you know..." Chip's absence is suddenly felt even stronger among them, as Woody continues to plead his case. "We need everyone else here to fly *our* planes, when the winds eventually calm."

Frederick purses his lips, remains momentarily silent, and then glances around at his tight-knit assembly of fire-pilots. As a final point, Woody comments, "I'm not much help here on the ground, but I can still be pretty useful in the air."

Looking over at Camille, who still appears unwilling, Frederick nods his reluctant consent. "Okay, Woody... You will act as flight engineer with Flynn being pilot-in-command and Floyd in the copilot seat." Camille holds her tongue and, with a click of her pen, keeps silent as the Old Man continues. "I want Sam and Chuck on standby with the chopper, if the safety clearance comes in for more air-drops." Spirits lifted with the relaxing of tension in the room, Woody is temporarily brought back into the fold of airmen. Their leader looks to each one of them and then comments, "Okay, fellas... You know what we're up against and what has to be done. Flynn, you better get your crew over to Pocatello and be ready for when those big tankers come in."

Flynn and Floyd go to leave, and Woody hangs back. Appreciative, he looks to his supervisor with a warm smile. "Thank you, old friend."

Frederick nods and waves him off. "Go on, Woody... Go and do what you do best."

When Woody follows after the others toward the stairs, Camille hurries behind and calls out to them. "Mister Russell, can I talk with you a moment?"

Stepping aside to let the others pass, Flynn watches them as they go downstairs. Camille takes his arm and pulls him away to the corner of the room. She speaks in a low whisper. "I don't think you understand what you've volunteered for."

He looks at her strangely and replies, "What is it exactly that's bothering you?" Hearing the doors bang as the others go outside, he moves to follow after them. "This isn't my first time in the big tankers."

She keeps a tight grip on his arm and holds him back. "I know that. The reports on these wildfires are very serious. There is a lot of dead timber in some of those areas, and the hot, dry winds have things whipped into a fierce fire-storm." She studies his features, hoping for a reaction, but gets none. "They're hoping that some of them will burn the others out, but I think they're only letting things intensify."

Taking a look around at the room's brisk activity, trying to tune out the unceasing chatter and ringing phones, Flynn stares straight at his former wife and directly asks her, "What is your *worry* here, Camille?"

"The ground-crews are in serious need of air support, and they're going to send you guys in as soon as conditions are even close to marginal. Whoever makes that judgement call will try not to compromise your safety, but it will be weighed against the risks of the boots on the ground."

Fire Angels

He nods his understanding and is a little off-put, until he notices a glimmer of concern in her usually hard features. "That's nice... You miss me already?"

Her hint of concern quickly fades, and the hard-nosed corporate woman returns with, "Dammit! You're *impossible*! Get your ass out of here, and don't you crack up any expensive airplanes!"

"That's why you have *insurance*, isn't it?"

Her irritation continues to rise as she barks at him. "Take care of your flight crew, and I will expect a full report upon your return." He affectionately pats her on the shoulder, grins, and leans in to whisper, "There's the hard-ass, ball-breaker I know and love."

She glares after him, as he steps away and bounds down the stairway to join the others waiting outside.

Chapter 31

On the highway leading to Pocatello, there is a heavy fog and a strong smell of smoke in the air. Flynn drives his Jeep, with Floyd sitting in the back seat and Woody riding shotgun. Strong gusts of wind occasionally blow against the vehicle, shifting it across the center line on the road.

On the passenger side, Woody examines the positions of the multiple fires on the aerial map opened across his lap, while Floyd has a look over his shoulder from the back seat. The acting flight engineer points to the map and comments, "The way these winds are swirling around, it is going to be hard to predict any kind of front lines."

Fish scoots forward, bracing himself between the forward headrests and grimaces. "Hell, most of the time, we're just spitting into the wind anyhow."

In his rearview mirror, Flynn glimpses at his crew. "With the wind blowing like it is today, I just hope we don't end up spitting in our own faces." Woody looks out the side window and then at Flynn, as the driver holds both hands to the steering wheel to combat the gusting wind. "Hey, Flynn... I was wondering... Have you ever flown big tankers in this kind of crazy weather?"

Flynn shrugs as another strong blast of wind scoots the Jeep all the way to the rumble strip at the edge its road lane.

"Sure... During my time in the Middle East, the wind and sand storms were legendary."

Holding a grab-handle in the back, Fish shouts forward, "Yeah, they're downright biblical."

Flynn looks over his shoulder to the rear of the Jeep, and smirks in reply. "Of course, I've never flown in these exact wind and fire conditions. It's a whole different ball-game maintaining controlled flight at two hundred feet over a landscape of flaming candlesticks."

Concerned, Woody shakes his head and looks back down at the topography map. "Well, these C-130s are pretty tough birds. They'll take a hell of a lot of punishment."

Flynn's gaze flits up to check the rearview mirror again. Sensing the crew's understandable nervousness, he replies, "Not a huge problem... We'll just be steering a flying brick house through the air over a Sunday barbecue."

Woody nods. "That puts a positive spin on it..."

~*~

Arriving at the airport in Pocatello, they observe a massive amount of fire-fighting resources at the air base. Checking in at the gate, the seconded team drives their vehicle to an assigned parking area filled with the dozens of other crew and fire-support vehicles. Despite being larger in scale, the station seems to be similar in setup to the Fire Angel base. Watching from the passenger-side window, Woody whistles through his teeth and murmurs, "It's been awhile since I was a part of an operation this big."

Parked, Flynn keeps the shifter in gear and shuts off the ignition. The wind rocks them slightly, and he looks back at his crew. "Well, boys, we're not the first ones on the scene."

Floyd laughs and slaps Woody's shoulder. "Better to be late to the party than missing it."

Fire Angels

The men exit the vehicle, grab their gear bags out of the back and make their way to the epicenter of the activity. Emergency vehicles and crew are everywhere. As they walk past a lineup of smaller aircraft, they watch ground-crews hastily tie down the airplanes to secure them against the strong winds.

The afternoon sky glows burnt-orange, and the clouds are tinted with a brown haze of smoke from the forest fires miles away. The thundering roar of approaching airplanes overhead grabs their attention and sends a shiver of goose-flesh up Flynn's arms. They gaze skyward, as two enormous C-130 tankers fly past the airport. Flynn laughingly observes, "Either they're leaving without us, or they just arrived."

Stopped in their tracks, they watch the final landing approach of the first big airplane as it comes thundering in. The huge airplane crabs sideways against the strong winds. Rough blasts of air toss it around like a child's toy, as it drops in over the runway. Finally, with the sound of rubber tires skidding, the rear set of wheels touch pavement. The big tanker aircraft settles into a straight line and races down the landing strip.

The next C-130 comes in at the same angled approach, but a down-flow draft of air shoves it toward the ground too fast, and it countermeasures by pulling up for another go-around. Awestruck, Flynn comments aloud, "That's a whole lot of airplane to pull out quick with."

Whistling through his teeth again, Woody watches the military surplus aircraft roar over their heads and murmurs, "They are some big wonderful birds!"

Holding onto one of his paperback romance novels, Floyd laughs apprehensively and slaps the book on his thigh. "I'm guessing I won't get much reading done up there…"

Gazing skyward, Flynn watches the air tanker come around again, crabbing sideways into the intermittent winds. "You'll probably get more than enough wait and read time on the ground, until conditions improve enough for us to fly."

The oversized aircraft, with its US Forest Service logos, finally lands and thunders down the runway. Flynn's flight crew makes their way through the massive assembly of fire-fighters and emergency equipment, and continues on to the command center for check-in.

~*~

On the dense forest floor, below billowing columns of smoke, the fires steadily sweeps through the woods, jumping from tree to tree, without restraint. With every breath of blowing wind, the inferno intensifies. Fire crews on the ground are in constant retreat, as the raging wildfire continues to push them back from the weakly established front line.

Chapter 32

At the Pocatello base, firefighters, pilots and ground-crew are crowded into a holding area waiting for their specific orders. Next to Floyd, Flynn lounges relaxed, in spite of the activity, in a chair with his eyes closed, attempting to catch a snooze. His eyes flutter open, and he gets a glimpse of the copilot reading from his bodice-buster paperback.

Fish chuckles quietly to himself and turns a page. Unable to sleep, Flynn opens his eyes again and peers over. "You get to a juicy part?"

The copilot grins, as he puts his finger between the pages to hold his spot. "Yeah, the writing is terrible, but the situation is fantastic." Glancing over to Flynn, Fish loudly whispers, "Hey, Flynn… You ever been married?"

Flynn, lets his eyelids drift closed again as he replies, "Marriage and romance are both expensive ways to watch someone slowly despise you."

Fish closes his paperback with his finger inside to mark his place, and snorts at Flynn. "Is that what's happening with you and the new corporate ball-buster?"

Flynn's eyes jut open, and he sits up. He is taken aback at the sudden reveal of what he thought was a well-kept secret. "What do you mean, Fish?"

"From reading this stuff, I know all about how it works. Who could have missed that look she gave when you put your hand up to volunteer for this one?"

"What...? She *did*?"

"Heck, I read more than my share of mushy-romance, but I don't think I'm the only one who noticed it."

There is a buzz of commotion from the command center, and Woody, with a nervous look on his face, steps out. He walks up to where Flynn and Floyd are seated and hands them each a clipboard, pen, and papers to be signed. Flynn tries to read the worry on the man's features and asks, "What's up, Woody?"

"They want us to in the air, but conditions out there are pretty terrible at best." Woody looks outside, away from them. "We saw those tankers come in sideways just a few hours ago, and things aren't much improved." Overly pensive, he is reluctant to say more.

Puzzled by Woody's reticent behavior, Flynn asks, "What else?"

"There's a unit of Hotshots near the lake trying to work themselves out of a tight situation." Troubled, Woody looks outside again, where strong winds rock the tied-down wings of grounded aircraft.

Flynn glances over the official forms attached to the clipboard and asks, "What do they want us to do?"

Brought back to attention, Woody takes a deep breath. "They're thinking, if we can get in close with a tanker drop, it could make the difference for them."

Floyd claps his book closed and looks to the clipboard and paperwork on his lap. "Where do we sign up?" Fish looks up and taps his book on Woody's leg. "What the hell are we waiting for?" He smiles at Flynn. "Fire Angels to the rescue!!"

Fire Angels

Adjusting his fire & wing, lucky cap, Flynn cracks a grin and signs the first page of the release forms. Giving a reassuring nod to Woody, he comments, "Birds of a feather…"

~*~

Lining up on the Pocatello flight strip, the two C-130 tankers warm their engines. Flight crews complete their preflight checklists while the propellers spin at an idle. Rumbling engines, pairs on each wing operate smoothly. Strong, smoke-tainted winds blow a cloudy haze across the base, pushing against parked vehicles and tethered aircraft.

~*~

Inside the cockpit of the Forest Service C-130 tanker, Flynn sits behind the expansive bank of controls, finishing his preflight check. He completes this required procedure and glances out the side windows to the whirling propellers on each wing to visually verify operation. He turns his attention forward, as the other airplane throttles up its engines, readying for takeoff. In the copilot position, Floyd, with his romance novel firmly tucked between his knees, double-checks the preflight list. Flynn waits for his copilot's approval before glancing back to Woody in the flight engineer's spot. "All set, Woody?"

"Check, Captain. Just a walk in the park…"

Fish adjusts his headset microphone and chimes in, "On a windy, windy day…"

Flynn stares ahead through the window, as the other tanker starts to roll forward adding, "And the park is on fire."

The Fire Angel crew waits on standby, observing as the loaded C-130 before them throttles up and charges down the runway to lift off. With the wings canted severely to the side, it struggles to take flight. Separating from the tarmac, the wheels bark as the aircraft banks into the wind.

The next C-130 revs its engines and crawls forward to line up on the runway. Stiff gusts of crosswind blow intermittently against the sides of the stout tanker, tilting the aircraft and fluttering the wingtips. Gradually, all four of the engines throttle up to full power. The wheel brakes release, and the loaded water tanker races down the airstrip.

Spinning propellers pull the aircraft forward, until the lift under the broad wings steadily raises the vessel skyward. An unexpected updraft lifts the starboard wing and the opposite wingtip nearly scrapes along the grass median between the runways. Pulling up harder, the aircraft narrowly avoids cartwheeling on the ground and roars into the smoke-filled firmament.

Flynn levels out the wings and eases up on the yoke. He glances at his copilot, Floyd the Fish, who puts on a relieved grin and sighs. "That was exciting…"

The aircraft's intercom crackles to life, and Woody's voice comes over the speaker. "Well, fellas, that was the easy part of our day. Look what we're heading toward…"

Ahead, a wall of smoke and flames rises up from the glowing ridgeline on the mountainous horizon. As they join the lead air tanker, the big C-130s are silhouetted by the flames consuming the wilderness. Flynn runs a pointed finger along the edge of his cap brim and salutes his crew, as he grunts through the headset mic. "Some kind of angels we are, flying straight into hell."

Chapter 33

Surrounded by heavy smoke and burning timber, a group of fire-fighters work frantically to clear a line of defense. Trapped by a wall of flames, the supervisor uses the radio to make another emergency plea for help. "Hot-pants to base, this is crew number seventeen. We are en route to the lake. Can you advise on our relief situation?" The base controller responds. "Crew leader, keep on a heading of west by north to reach the lake. Surface fires are blocking all other exit routes. We will have to evacuate you by air when you get there."

The crew leader looks at the nearby shovel-wielding fire-fighters with sweaty, soot-covered faces. Then, he looks around to the other fire-suit clad figures frantically chopping and scratching at the underbrush, attempting to fend-off a wall of flame. He responds to base command. "Copy that... We will move toward the shoreline of the lake, and then reestablish radio contact and prepare for aerial evacuation."

The thunderous roar of the forest fire drowns out the crackling sound of the radio. Nearby, a flaming tree limb crashes to the ground, causing the fire-fighters to jump back and regroup. Turning to face his crew, the leader hollers at them and points northwest. "We've got to get to the lake. We're backed into a corner, and there is no other way out!" The group responds instantly and, through a canyon of flames, begins making its way toward the lake.

~*~

Observed from above, the wildfire quickly moves along the treetops, like candles on an octogenarian's birthday cake. The intermittent winds create a blast furnace of dry heat convection that pushes the whirling fingers of flame to lash out. The tree canopy seems to burst into flames instantly as the high temperatures of the atmosphere prove too much for the woodland's natural fire resistance.

Tucked between the burning mountains, a lake reflects a fierce orange glow, as the pair of C-130s banks toward it. Their metal skins shimmer eerily, as they approach. Competently, Flynn muscles the airplane along, following close behind the other air-tanker. Strong winds and heated updrafts lift and slam the aircraft like they were mere children's toys in the sky. Another jarring blast of turbulence smashes into Flynn's plane, rattling his teeth and forcing him to tighten his grip on the yoke.

The co-pilot puts his paperback novel aside and holds onto the airframe, as they endure the unrelenting jostling. Through the windshield, they all watch as the lead plane lifts, dips and dives, as it is slammed around by rough air currents. Fish tightens his lap belt strap, when he feels their aircraft lifted by an updraft and then, with a slamming jolt, dropped. His paperback novel momentarily floats upward and then tumbles to his feet. He kicks it aside and points to the fiery display ahead of them. "Hell fire... It feels about like it looks, and they're not faring much better."

They watch the lead C-130 desperately try to maintain its intended heading in spite of the wind. Clenching his teeth, Flynn grips the yoke firmly and responds, "And it's only gonna get worse... How we doing, Woody?"

Fire Angels

Holding tight to the bulkhead, Woody yells. "A bit of a rough ride fellas, but nothing this bird can't handle. I've been through way worse turbulence in Vietnam."

Fish peers back to Woody and humorously replies, "Back when you were our age?"

"Funny kid! Back then, people were shooting at us..." Their stomachs feel an odd lifting sensation, as the heavily-loaded water tanker dives with a forceful wind current, and then is abruptly slammed hard by another pocket of rising air. The airframe violently shudders, jarring the occupants and rattling every rivet in the plane's metal skin.

Flynn muscles the airplane back under control and charges ahead. "Damn! Didn't like that one much..."

Over the intercom, Woody's voice crackles loudly. "They want us to follow their lead... Come in low and splash a clear trail to the lake for those Hotshots."

Scanning the area, it is obvious that the raging wildfires have nearly converged around the lake, cutting off any other possible escape route. Flynn keeps both hands firmly planted on the bucking yoke, wrestling the wind as he speaks into his microphone. "Is the plan to get them out from the water?"

Woody's voice cracks in. "Too windy for the chopper... If things settle down just a bit, they could easily send the Catalina in to pick 'em up..."

The pilots do their damnedest to keep the aircraft under control in anticipation of their low-level flight. Propellers whirling, the four engines roar at a steady speed. Constant jolts of air current, from both above and below, smash into the plane, straining it to its limits.

~*~

On the ground, a dozen Hotshots skirt the edge of the inferno as they move through the forest. They look overhead at the sound of approaching air tankers that can be heard over

151

the roaring flames. Suddenly, the pair of airplanes soars past. The crew leader quickly gets on the radio and messages in. "We have a visual on the aircraft for the drop. Bring them in low on a heading of…" Before the communication is complete, an enormous tree, engulfed in flames, topples over. Commands and responses are muffled by the roar of the wildfire, as they are forced to maneuver around the obstruction that now blocks their path.

Chapter 34

The C-130 continues to be hammered by the strong winds and updrafts caused by the wildfires below. Flynn turns the yoke, tilts the plane's wings, and banks toward the lake. Looking out to the smoke and fire-filled horizon, his survival instinct kicks in, giving him a heavy surge of adrenaline.

When an emergency flare arcs through the sky, the aerial firefighting crew scans the area to pinpoint its origin. Near a toppled, flaming tree, a small cluster of men are spotted trying to work around it to gain access to a limited stretch of unburned forest near the lake. Flynn jabs a finger downward, as he hollers into his mic. "That's them there!"

Floyd the Fish, nodding in agreement, presses his cheek to the hot glass window. "I can see a few of them."

Banking the water tanker in a wide arc over the lake, Flynn follows along behind the other aircraft. Woody's voice comes over the radio. "They're going to put us on a course, and we can take up where they leave off."

"Copy that… Coming around now."

The water tankers come around on a return heading toward the lake. The lead C-130 dips down closer to the trees, as flames lick at its polished metal underbelly. Flying low and slow over the treetops, the drop tanks open to release a misting flood of red fire-retardant. The fire-fighting mixture blankets a wide trail halfway from the fallen tree to the lake.

The angry hiss of the wildfire is deafening, as the surrounding flames threaten to overtake the escape route. Hotshots scramble to keep close to the doused evacuation route, snaking single file through the timber. On the heels of the leading aircraft, the Fire Angels crew comes in behind to initiate its drop where the other left off.

~*~

The reflective shell of the C-130 glows brilliant orange, as Floyd and Flynn observe the airplane out ahead of them. The blanketing drop from the leading aircraft lasts only a few seconds but spreads sixty feet wide, a distance of a half mile. Woody's voice crackles through the radio. "They were right on target!" In spite of the noise of the engines and the wildfire, his next remark is loud and clear. "We just have to bring them the rest of the way to the lake."

Flynn dives the airplane closer to the flaming treetops, watching as the other tanker aircraft pulls out from their drop and climbs to a safer altitude. "Copy that... Heading into the thick of it now..."

The fuselage of the aircraft is pummeled from every direction, as hot currents of air rise from below. Flynn holds the yoke steady, attempting to ease their steep descent. Gripping the seat tightly between jarring blasts of turbulence, Floyd glances nervously at the pilot as they soar even lower. "How low we gonna go, pal?"

"Just a bit more..."

"We'll have to be sure to drop well ahead of their forward position, or we'll wash them out."

Consumed by fierce concentration, Flynn tilts his chin to respond, "We've got to sweep out any flames in their path, so they have a clear passage to the shore." Propellers churn the glowing embers like egg beaters raked through a campfire. Beads of sweat pouring from his brow, Flynn pushes to the

Fire Angels

lower limits of a safe drop-altitude and continues to dive. "Almost there…" There is a jolting slam against the airframe, as hot air currents shift dramatically when they pass over the path of the previous drop. Teeth clenched, Flynn glances over to Floyd. "Hold on… Not yet…"

~*~

The stranded Hotshot crew, on a heading to the lake, scrambles through the smoldering drop zone. They look overhead, as the second tanker flies past, barely above the treetops. In awe, the ground crew watches as the airplane skims dangerously low over the raging inferno.

~*~

Crashing through the flames, Flynn swiftly approaches the shoreline while keeping his eyes on his intended target. The aircraft buzzes the previous drop zone, as it charges forward. Flynn holds off a moment… Then, he calls out and signals the water tanks to be released. "Okay! Let 'er dump!!!"

In a surging rush, the contents of the tanker are released over the fiery terrain. The low flying plane instantly lightens and becomes more responsive, as two thousand seven hundred gallons of liquid retardant is quickly released through tubes at the rear cargo door. Glancing out his side window, Flynn can see the stranded crew on the ground raise their arms in cheering thanks, while scampering over charred debris toward the safety of the lake.

As the leading air tanker circles and turns, on a heading back toward the home base, the Fire Angel crew finishes the drop and then gains altitude over the lake, tinted dark-orange by the reflection of surrounding flames. Sweeping down from the mountains on the opposite shore, a powerful gust of wind fans the wildfire, whipping the flames into a column of fire and smoke. Suddenly, a fire tornado appears directly in the path of the airplane. Frantically pulling back on the yoke,

Flynn attempts to gain altitude to climb over the whirling dervish of flames, cursing to himself as Floyd shouts out, "Holy shit! What the hell is that?"

The strained engines of the C-130 roar, as the pilots struggle to pull up and away from the path of the flaming tornado. As they are about to be sucked into the spinning conflagration, Flynn heaves at the controls, groaning, "Dammit... We're gonna fly right into it!!"

~*~

With no time to climb to a higher altitude, the C-130 has little choice but to fly directly into the churning pillar of flames. Engulfed, it completely disappears. The crackling growl of the firestorm continues as waves of the water reflect the blazing inferno.

Chapter 35

Desperately, Flynn and Floyd struggle to gain control of the airplane, while Woody calls out to them through broken transmissions on the radio. "All systems are failing... Pull out now...!" The aircraft violently twists and turns, as a blanket of fire swirls around it. Woody's voice on the radio crackles in, "We're going down...!!!!"

Stall alarms beep and warning lights blink incessantly, as the airplane spirals into an uncontrollable flat spin. The heat inside the cockpit is becoming unbearable, and the crew tries to brace themselves on any surface of the cockpit that isn't blazing hot. Surprisingly, Fish directs one of his goofy grins toward Flynn, accepting their imminent fate, and remarks, "Dorothy, I don't think we're in Kansas anymore!"

Drenched in sweat, Flynn exerts all the control he can, as he continues to fly the aircraft, all the way to the ground. Over the din of the raging tornado, he hollers to his crew, "We've lost the main controls! Nothing is responding..."

The number two engine explodes into a ball of flames, and Floyd is quick to hit the extinguisher button to choke-out the fuel to the engine. He looks to Woody in the rear of the cockpit and then to Flynn before hollering, "Anything else we can do here, Captain?"

"We're not done yet!"

"You mean *cooked well-done*?!?"

Flynn grins with determination. "We still have power to the other engines. Let's fly this bird until we can't..."

Fish looks back to the flashing lights on the control panel and snaps off a salute. "Aye aye, Captain!"

~*~

The swirling fire tornado picks up flaming debris, as it travels through the burning forest along the lakefront. Enveloped by the freak occurrence, the aircraft spins like a top over the treetops, which are lit up like a Viking funeral pyre. One after another, the airplane's engines explode with a popping burst of flames. The shiny metal skin of the plane glows red hot, as the painted Forest Service logo crinkles and then burns away. Under tremendous strain, melted rivets begin to fail, and sheets of metal separate from the airframe. At the mercy of a powerful force of nature, the large aircraft is tossed like a toy in a whirlpool.

~*~

As the windshield begins to buckle and crack from the heat, Flynn looks to his crew of longtime friends and is strangely at peace with their mutual fate. Proudly, he watches them keeping to task in an attempt to gain control of the crashing airplane. For a brief moment, the surface of the lake can be seen through the wall fire ahead. Its shimmering, orange waves seem to beckon the fiery chariot in.

Nearly passed-out from the heat and velocity of the g-force, Floyd, jabbing a finger at the window, yells to Flynn. "We still have power to the number four engine!"

Trying to steer them out of the spin, Flynn pulls back and cranks the yoke while calling back, "Aim for the lake!" The plane is at the mercy of the swirling tornado, as they both yank at the unresponsive flight controls. There is a sudden break, as they reach the eye of the storm, and the spinning aircraft slingshots out and away from the funnel of flames.

Fire Angels

~*~

Making their way to the safety of the lake, the ground-crew watches the big C-130 aircraft shoot out of the fire tornado as if spit from the belly of a beast. Flames flick out from the engine cowlings, and the metal wings are ablaze. Sideways, the flaming aircraft hits the lake creating a tremendous splash that snaps the tail section free and crumples a sizzling wing over the top of the broken fuselage. Steam hisses from the wreckage as it bobs briefly at the water's surface, before it slowly begins to sink. The cockpit windows shimmer, illuminated by the surrounding wildfires, as the forward section tips to the side and goes under.

Gathered along the shore, the Hotshot crew stands in awed reverence, staring out at the floating remains of the fire-bombing aircraft. One of the crew removes his helmet to honor the sacrifice made in the effort to save them. With the forest fire raging behind them, the rest of the crew repeats the gesture, some lowering their gaze in prayer.

Suddenly, the low rumbling roar of an approaching PBY Catalina is heard. In response to the aircraft's arrival, eyes lift skyward, and smiles break through soot-covered features. Skirting the treetops, the amphibious rescue aircraft dumps a load of fire-retardant mixture before skimming over the glowing lake for a water-landing.

~*~

At the Fire Angel headquarters, the whole command center is quiet, as Frederick stands next to the radio controls with a downcast expression on his face. He lifts the receiver again and speaks, holding back strong emotions. "Copy that. Complete your rescue pickup of the Hotshot crew and scan the wreckage for survivors."

Behind him, with a faraway expression hiding her heartache, Camille stares at the lights of the radio console.

Slowly, she turns away and directs her attention out the window to the airplanes and assembled crews of firefighters. Everyone in the office remains hushed, as they quietly mourn the tragic loss of life.

Putting down the radio receiver, the Old Man croaks, "Back to work everyone. There are still fires to be put out." Stoically, he watches everyone resume their tasks. He moves to stand by Camille at the window and follows her gaze outside. Clearing the rising lump in his throat, he murmurs, "They say the winds are calming down some."

She tries to blink away the tears glistening in her eyes. "I'll have Chuck up in the air as soon as we get the all-clear." They both watch to the horizon, where the glowing clouds of smoke color the sky over the forest fires many miles away. Jaw quivering, Frederick gets control of his feelings and states, "This has been one of the worst ones I've seen in a long time."

Staring forward, Camille nods her head and takes a breath. "It figures... We now have as many contracts as we could possibly handle but not enough pilots to fly them."

He gives her a fleeting look and then adds, reluctantly, "We *do* have another experienced flyer that can get up there..."

Chapter 36

The surface of the lake mirrors the image of flames consuming the wooded shoreline. Perched at the edge of the water with the tail above the shore, the PBY Catalina's engines idle with the propellers spinning while the last of the fire-fighting crew is loaded aboard. Straight ahead, in the lake, a lone wingtip of the C-130 fire-bomber is seen jutting from the water's surface.

With all aboard, the Catalina's rear-hatch door finally closes, and the twin radial engines throttle up. Props whirling, the seaplane pulls ahead onto the fire-reflected water and taxies toward the submerged wreckage. It solemnly pauses at the crash site before continuing. At the opposite shore, the seaplane readies for takeoff, pivoting around to face out to the longest stretch of water

Moving forward at full throttle, water pushes aside and the propellers whirl like gleaming discs of glass. The seaplane races across the lake, and splashes of water curl away from the flying-boat hull. As they cruise past the submerged wreckage, the engines roar and the aircraft lifts from the water's surface. The seaplane flies across the lake, rises over the flaming trees, and banks away to the south.

~*~

At the Fire Angel headquarters, the PV2 Harpoon taxies over to the airstrip with Chuck seated at the controls.

He twists his head to look over his shoulder, watching as the OV-10A Bronco taxies up behind him. His preflight check completed, Chuck stares down the empty runway, engages the wheel brakes, and throttles up his engine.

"Chuck here, to *Bronco*. You ready for this?"

The radio crackles for a minute, until the Old Man's voice booms back. "You bet I am! Had to dust off my wings and find my jacket, but I'll be right up there with you to guide us into the drop."

Seated at the controls of the Bronco spotter plane, Frederick brings the aircraft into position behind the water-bomber already faced out to the runway. He watches the aircraft leap forward, as the brakes on the Harpoon release. The water tanker moves swiftly down the strip and lifts off. With a grunt, the Old Man adjusts the settings on his flight controls and murmurs. "There's no fool like an old fool."

From the office window, Camille observes as the Bronco charges down the airstrip and then climbs into the sky, following after the twin-tailed PV2 Harpoon. As she watches them fly off to the north, the airplanes fly in formation, becoming silhouettes in the sky. Her thoughts return to Flynn and his eternal love of flying. Lips quivering, she sighs and wipes a streak of tears from her cheek.

The sound of resumed activity in the room wakes her from contemplation. Turning to the staff, she calls out. "Okay, listen up people...! Let's get a handle on this burn. We need good communication to guide them in to their drop zones, and then get them safely back home to the nest"

~*~

The PBY Catalina flies over the mountainous terrain toward the Fire Angel air base. Behind them, the wildfires continue to spew dark, billowing clouds of smoke skyward. The pilot in in command, Kansas Sam, speaks into his headset mic as he looks back to the crew of filthy, fire-fighters packed inside the plane's cargo hold. "This is Catalina Two-Twenty. Water drop was completed successfully, and we have the Hotshot crew all picked up and accounted for. We are now headed back home."

"What is the status on the downed C-130?"

Sam turns in his seat to face forward. Looking to the clear horizon, he steers the seaplane through the mountainous terrain. He somberly replies, "The aircraft is a total loss... Have an emergency medical team standing by for our arrival in approximately forty minutes." The drone of the engines sets a mournful tone, and Sam glances back to the rescued group again. Then, returning his attention to the controls, he continues to follow the flight path to the Fire Angel air base.

~*~

Leading the way, Frederic flies the Bronco over the wildfire site and peels away to climb to a higher altitude. Behind him, after angling in a steep, water-bombing dive, Chuck levels-off to pilot the PV-2 Harpoon low over the fire. Almost looking as if the plane will land on the fiery treetops, the aircraft, at the last moment, drops a billowing path of fire-retardant over the forest fire.

The Old Man's encouraging voice comes on the radio. "Nice drop, Chuck! Right on target. Couldn't have done it better myself!"

Wiping the sweat that streams down his temples, Chuck laughs and replies, "Who ya think I learned it from?"

Frederick responds cheerfully. "Let's head for home and fill-up for another run."

"Copy that, Old Man. I will follow your lead."

The two firefighting planes bank away from the flaming conflagration and fly back toward headquarters.

Chapter 37

Sporadic blasts of wind blow across the airfield at base headquarters. The wind sock can't seem to find direction, as it lifts, drops and swings around again to stand out straight. Entering the valley, the PBY Catalina approaches the airstrip. A sudden updraft lifts the left wingtip, and the amphibious plane rights itself before coming in for a wheeled landing. Taxiing to the end of the landing field, the water-bomber pivots on a braked wheel and rolls toward the hangar. Quickly on the scene, several emergency vehicles pull up behind with their red and blue lights flashing.

In the upper office of the headquarters building, Camille stands at the window watching the Catalina's arrival. Unintentionally, she holds her breath a brief moment, as the airplane rolls to a stop and then finally cuts its engines. Emergency crew members with medical equipment pour out of their vehicles and rush to the rear hatch of the seaplane to help the rescued fire-fighters disembark. She looks to the medical stretchers lined up and waiting on the field and can't help but hope for everyone's survival. Considering the odds, and having been in the military almost her entire career, she understands the foolishness of wishing. To keep appearances, Camille takes a breath, pulls her shoulders back and glances around the office.

After a crackle of static from the radio console beside her, she hears Frederick's voice come through the speakers. "Bronco and Harpoon here... We're on our way in to refuel and refill the drop tanks. All clear to land?"

The radio controller clicks the receiver and responds, "Fire Angel runway is clear for landing. Come on home."

Sucking in a breath, Camille turns back to the window, watching intently as a body, wrapped in a blanket, is carried from the aircraft and placed on a stretcher. From the window, the distance is too great to make out the clear features of any of the disembarking crew. She glances over at a pair of binoculars on the desk, but reconsiders when she hears the other airplanes approaching.

Coming over the horizon, dropping from the sky, the Bronco comes in for a landing, followed by the Harpoon. Camille watches the loaded stretcher get tucked away in the back of an ambulance and cannot contain herself any longer. Consumed by emotion, Camille lets out her held breath and breaks for the stairway.

~*~

Hurrying down the stairs, Camille dashes toward the exit. She is about to charge through the double screen doors, when one side opens to reveal a rumpled, water-soaked and slightly bloodied Flynn Russell. Her high heels skid to a halt on the plank floor, and she stares at him with complete surprise. Flynn adjusts his Fire Angels cap over his wet, messy hair and puts on a jovial grin. "What's your hurry, Darlin'? Coming out to see about me... or just to find out if the airplane is okay?"

The screen door slams shut behind him, and Camille suddenly finds herself rushing into his open arms. She buries her face in his chest and then pulls back to face him. No words are exchanged. Flynn pulls her to him and gives her a deep, passionate kiss. At length, she breaks from the kiss and pries herself from his grasp. With concern, she wipes the tears from her cheeks and asks, "How are the other guys?"

The sound of an exaggerated throat clearing comes from behind Flynn, and the other door swings open when Fish pops his head inside. Displaying his signature goofy grin, he looks at Flynn and shrugs. "Was nice of her to ask about us. Somehow, I don't think I'm gonna get the same welcome-home greeting, though…"

Flynn peels away from his embrace with Camille and gestures to his copilot. "If it wasn't for Fish here, swimming down and pulling us out, we would all still be sitting in that melting aircraft, and all out of air bubbles." Camille takes a step back from Flynn, when she notices Floyd's bandages and the sling cradling his arm. "Are you hurt badly?"

"They say I probably tore a tendon or something in my shoulder, when it dislocated during the crash landing."

In astonishment, Camille looks at Flynn and then back to Floyd. "You swam them out with a dislocated arm?" Sucking in his cheeks, Fish puckers his lips like his namesake. "The only thing I'm better at than flying, is swimming."

Thankful for their return, Camille then remembers their flight engineer and asks, hesitantly, "What about Woody…?"

Flynn looks outside toward the circus of emergency vehicles and medical personnel tending to the rescued Hotshots. "Woody got torn-up pretty bad, but we think he'll be okay. He has a broken leg and hip. Some busted ribs, probably… They're taking him to the hospital for surgery."

Stepping inside, moving past Flynn and Camille, Fish holds out his sopping-wet paperback romance novel and shakes it. He pats Flynn on the shoulder in passing, and smirks toward Camille. "I could be reading things all wrong, but she didn't rush into my arms…"

Flynn grins appreciatively, as Camille quickly makes the transformation back into her uptight business demeanor. She coughs to clear her throat and gestures to Floyd's arm. "I'm guessing that with your injured shoulder, you won't be airborne anytime soon?"

Fish puts on his familiar, ludicrous grin and retorts, "Faster than a sling-chicken!"

Camille stares at him, not understanding his weird sense of humor. Glancing at Flynn before addressing Floyd again, she states, "Tell Sam to start his report on the rescue operation and to see me in the office as soon as he can." Moving back toward the stairway, she calls over her shoulder. "It's *all hands on deck*... Every available air tanker is being fueled and outfitted. They'll be out within the hour."

Flynn sighs and nods. "Good... We'll be ready."

Camille stops at the stairway and turns to look at Flynn. She assesses his tousled appearance, noticing a smear of blood coming from a wound above his eye, and remarks, "I'm glad you made it out okay, but the both of you are grounded until an investigation of the incident is complete."

With a look of angry frustration filling his features, Flynn stares at Camille and growls, "We have drops that need to be made, and we're short on pilots who can make them." She merely stares back at him and he utters, "Are you serious? I can't be grounded right now!"

The businesswoman shakes her head disapprovingly and turns on a heel, heading up the stairs to the main office. She glances back at Flynn and responds, "Can't be helped. That's the way it is when you crack one up."

At the notion of being grounded, Flynn yells after her. "*I* didn't crack it up! We were sucked into a fire tornado and thrown out across that damn lake!" Midway up the staircase, she stops to look back at the two pilots.

Fire Angels

"Fire tornado?"

Flynn realizes the absurdity of what it sounds like. Calming himself so he doesn't sound irrational, he replies. "Yeah, it was a real freak of nature... Not our fault."

"Where is your airplane, Mister Russell?"

He grits his teeth and looks at Floyd before answering. "At the bottom of the lake by now, I guess."

She lifts both eyebrows, nods her head in a smug way and states, "If you don't bring the airplane back in one piece, you don't get to fly again until the report clears Air Safety."

Floyd shrugs his shoulder, wincing from the effort. "Sorry, pal... We did the best we could."

"Dammit... This is bullshit!"

Camille calls down to them, as she continues up the stairs. "Welcome back to the *real world*, boys..."

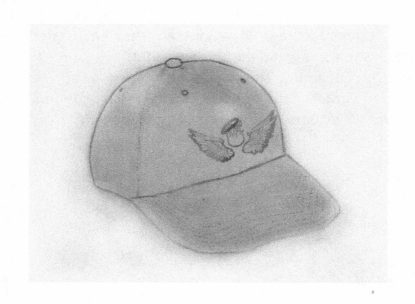

Chapter 38

As Camille makes her way up the stairs, the double screen doors open and the Old Man, followed by Chuck, appears. The expression of relief on both of their faces tells everything. The old aviator wraps his arm around Flynn's shoulder, pulling him in for a hug. "Flynn, my boy... How are you?"

"I'm fine, thanks."

Frederick releases the embrace and looks across the room to where Camille has stopped near the top of the stairs. "That's good to hear! Go get cleaned up, 'cause we need you in the air again if you're up for it."

Flynn, with a haughty look on his face, looks from the Old Man over to Camille at the top of the stairs and replies, "I'll be ready in five."

Descending a few steps, Camille puts on her most authoritative tone and addresses all of them in the room. "They should both be grounded until the NTSB has time to investigate the incident."

The Old Man stands up straighter and puts on his own commanding tone. "The proper authorities have been notified, so until the suits show up to say different, it's up to us to say if they can fly or not."

The corporate businesswoman looks at the owner of the Fire Angel operation, and there is an uncomfortable pause. She lets her eyes travel to each of the pilots looking up at her.

Shaking her head, Camille returns her stare to Frederick. "We'll see what the corporate office has to say about this."

The Old Man looks to Chuck and then over to Flynn, who lifts an eyebrow in reaction, and then back at Camille. "You tell them I'm the one running the show down here... And I will continue to do so, my way, until our contract is completed or retracted." Emasculated in front of the group, Camille turns away from them without responding and marches upstairs. The Old Man turns to look at the bandaged sling on Floyd's arm and waves at him to follow. "C'mon Fish, you can come with me. I'll need your help with coordinating things in the air." He turns and smiles at Flynn. "If you think you're up for it, I need as many pilots in the air as we've got, if we want to stay in business."

Flynn nods his absolute approval and turns to Chuck. "Hey, buddy... I guess we have some tankers to get in order."

Before Flynn steps out, the Old Man calls after him. "Flynn..."

Looking back, Flynn looks to his friend and mentor. "Yeah?"

Frederick sweeps back his silver hair and continues. "I'm really glad you made it today. You had us worried a bit."

Flynn smiles back, grateful. "Thanks."

The Old Man points a finger in the pilot's direction. "Take the Catalina up, and log as many water drops you can before we run out of daylight."

A wider smile crosses Flynn's features, and he snaps off a salute. "Yes, Sir!"

The screen doors slap shut as Flynn exits. The Old Man looks to Floyd. "How are ya, Fish?"

"Just glad we're still alive."

The Old Man huffs a tired breath and turns to go up the stairway. "Yeah... Me too..."

Fire Angels

~*~

The afternoon sky is a hazy, burnt-orange color, due to the heavy wildfire smoke that hangs in the atmosphere. Exiting the wide hangar doors, Flynn looks over at the shiny, black Mercedes car parked in front of the office. Cleaned up, with his hair slicked back and a bandage on his forehead, Flynn looks almost as good as before the crash.

He walks over to the PBY Catalina, briefly looks it over and greets the mechanic that climbs out of its rear hatch. "How's she lookin', Wing Nut?"

"After that last flight, Kansas Sam said she was like wrestling a greased pig at a Sunday cookout. With that wind tossing her about, we figure things are in tip-top shape."

Flynn pats Wing Nut on the back as the mechanic descends from the access hatch. "If you didn't have to muscle her around some, it wouldn't feel like flying."

The mechanic touches his hand to the metal skin of seaplane and laughs in agreement. He looks at the bandage on Flynn's head and asks, "How are you and the other fellas after the incident?"

"Fine, fine... Well... Woody is in surgery now and will hopefully be okay... And, Fish popped his damned arm off, but I'm ready to go back at it for another round of pissing on some forest fires."

Wing Nut steps away from the plane and looks up at the thick pylon that connects to the high-wing above the body. "Fuel is topped-off, so you should have more go-juice than daylight. Water tanks are filled, and the scoopers are in good order if you can get into that lake."

"Thanks, pal. We'll see how many runs we can get in before it gets dark." The aircraft mechanic watches the enthusiastic pilot climb up into the seaplane. Taking a few steps back, he then looks beyond to Chuck readying the lead

Bronco and to Kansas Sam pre-flighting the Harpoon. Returning his attention to the Catalina, Wing Nut assesses the vintage aircraft and gives a wave to Flynn in the cockpit. Receiving an affirmative thumbs-up gesture in return, the mechanic heads back to the hangar.

Flynn gets settled into the pilot's chair, repositions the fit of his hat and pulls the headphones over it. From the lower right side of his chair, he lifts the clip-board with its attached preflight checklist, clicks his pen and gets to work.

Chapter 39

With a bang, the doors of the office burst open and Camille rushes out. Through the cockpit window of the Catalina, she spots Flynn at the controls. Running in high heels, she makes her way to the seaplane, as the engines fire up and the propellers slowly begin to turn. Waving her arms overhead, she tries to get Flynn's attention.

Noticing her, Flynn turns from the controls to give her a curt salute. The propellers continue to spin as Camille stands beneath the left-side window and puts her hands on her hips in obvious protest. When he motions for her to step aside, she shakes her head and remains stationary to block his path.

Eventually, the overhead engines choke-out, and the propellers begin to wind down as Flynn cuts the power. Peering down at Camille, he shakes his head disapprovingly. He motions a finger for her to wait and pulls off his headset. Ducking away, Flynn momentarily disappears from her view. The rear hatch cracks open, and he confronts Camille.

"What is it, woman?!?"

"I'm leaving!"

Flynn looks back to the cockpit and then, with a nod of his head, back to Camille. "So am *I*."

Annoyed, she rolls her eyes at him and continues. "No… I talked with the corporate investment board, and they want to exercise a termination of the buyout."

Unsure of the consequences of this news, Flynn pauses and then hops down from the hatch. He gives her a look. "What does that mean for us?"

"The bean-counters don't foresee enough profit in the way things are going, which means that you and the Old Man are free and clear to run this little operation into the ground any way you see fit."

He shakes his head. *"No... That's not what I meant..."* He looks earnestly at her. "What's it mean for you and me?"

"You can stay here and go up in your beloved airplane, because there isn't a *you and me*." A fleeting hint of sadness is quickly replaced by her practiced expression of rigidity. "Tomorrow I'm gone, and I won't be around to deal with the government suits from NTSB with all their redundant questions and bullshit paperwork." Not knowing what to do, Flynn stares at her for a minute before reaching out to her. Putting on a brave face, she steps back. "This time, *I'm* the one leaving *you* for a job. They're going to assign me to supervise a San Diego charter outfit that is about to go under."

In obvious disappointment, Flynn casts his gaze downward. Camille responds by adopting a cool façade. Swallowing her emotions, she comments, "Don't get all sentimental on me now, Flynn. This is the life we signed-up for, and that's the way things go."

Biting his lower lip, he looks straight at her and nods. "I'm sorry things didn't work out this time, Camille."

"Yeah... Me, too."

He adds, "I thought you'd come by the cabin for another visit..."

She shrugs her shoulders, exhales, and forces a grin. "Hey, we're only good for about one or two weeks anyhow." Her expression almost cracks, but she sucks it up and states,

Fire Angels

"Look at it this way… You can fly away and do your thing without any strings attached. Go on, and do what you love."

With a sad expression, he gives her a coy wink. "It's the only thing I'm really good at."

"Yeah… Playing husband wasn't really your thing."

"With *you*, I didn't mind it all that much."

Camille puts on a genuine smile and waves him off. "Hell… You only live once, Fly-boy."

He tries to return her smile, but instead turns to the Catalina and the other fire-bombers warming their engines. He pauses to take a breath and then pivots to face her again. "Nah, you can only *die* once. You have to *live* every day." Stepping the short distance to her, he wraps her in his arms. She doesn't resist much, when he presses his mouth to hers. They embrace in a passionate kiss, until the engines of nearby aircraft begin to rev up for takeoff. Remembering his duties, Flynn releases Camille and, in a heart-felt goodbye, he states, "Maybe next time we'll work out…"

She shrugs, as she straightens her blouse and smirks. *"Third time's the charm…."*

"Yeah, third time lucky…" After a lingering look, he breaks away and turns back to his airplane. Climbing up through the hatch, he glances back at her as she gives a goodbye wave. He continues into the cargo hold and swings the door shut behind him. Situating himself behind the flight controls, Flynn starts the engines again. Hoping to see Camille's face one more time, he looks out his side window, but he only sees her attractive backside swooshing away as she walks toward the office. Thinking he might call out to her, his hand goes to slide open the window, but he stops himself. As she leaves, without looking back, he gives her a salute. "See ya, Honey…" Flynn pushes the dual throttles forward, pivots the rumbling airplane on one braked wheel and taxies toward the runway.

~*~

The commotion around the air base is punctuated by the loud roar of airplanes taking off. The Bronco charges down the runway, followed by the Harpoon and then, finally, the Catalina. They all lift into the sky, bank toward the smoky-orange glow on the horizon, and then, after arranging themselves in aerial formation, head off to do their work.

Chapter 40

Through smoke-laden skies, the fire-fighting aircraft fly toward mountains that glow with fire. Chuck's voice comes over the radio. "We're gonna attack the site that the Old Man and I dropped on earlier today... But, this time we're gonna come in from the east." As the experienced team flies their planes in tight formation, Chuck's radio message continues. "After the dump, we'll do a fly-over at the other location to survey the situation there, and Flynn's Catalina will do water scoops from the lake and make drops while we return to base to refill our water tanks."

Flynn is comfortable behind the controls of his favorite plane. He smiles, and pushes the microphone closer to his lips. "Copy that, good Buddy!"

The radio crackles with loud static then broadcasts Kansas Sam's voice. "Hey Flynn, ol' boy..." He chuckles. "Watch out for that C-130 that someone parked in the middle of your water runway..."

Flynn can't help but laugh, as he nods and replies, "Thanks for the pickup and rescue, Sam. Fish and I were sure thinking of you while spinning around in that fire-tornado, headed for Oz."

The radio crackles back. "Yeah, Dorothy... I bet that was one hell of a hot ride for you and Toto!"

Flynn retorts, joking, "Not the coolest ride in the park… I definitely wouldn't recommend it."

Chuck's voice cuts in. "Okay, boys… We're coming up on the drop zone now… Continue on that fire line to the south, and we'll hit it along the flank."

Smoke and tall licks of flame tint the sky with an orange radiance, as the airplanes dive at the wildfire below. With sparks and embers drifting skyward, the water-bombers come in low, one at a time, to drop their extinguishing loads.

~*~

Leading the way, Kansas Sam, in the Harpoon, dives in low just over the treetops. Cruising at about a hundred feet, he triggers the bomb-bay doors and dumps a wide-splashing spray of water and fire-retardant. He whirls his hand over his head like a rodeo bull-rider and screams out, "Whooohee…" The engines roar, as the aircraft pulls up and banks away from the intense heat. Over the radio, Sam calls, "The load is delivered, and I'm heading for home to refill. See you boys!"

Chuck's voice joins in on the radio, as he circles above. "Good drop, Sam. Right on target! Fill 'er up again and radio-in when you're on the return."

"Copy that." The Harpoon wags its wingtips and roars off to the south.

Following the same dive-path that Sam took the PBY Catalina lines up for its drop. Focused on the wildfire ahead, Flynn gradually pushes the aircraft into a steep dive toward the burning forest. He glances up through the glass canopy toward Chuck's spotter plane, before he redirects his attention to his meteoric rush over the flaming trees.

The plane roars over the treetops, dipping and diving through the convection currents created by the blazing heat. Sweating, Flynn adjusts the Fire Angel cap beneath his headset as he muscles the yoke. The sound of the engines, backed by the roaring firestorm, is deafening. Chuck's steady voice over the radio becomes part of the background noise. "Good line, Flynn... Keep on that mark... Almost there..."

As sweat streams down his forehead, Flynn blinks the stinging drips from his eyes and continues to struggle through the hot wind currents. Jaw tightly clenched, he replies into the radio mic. "Copy that... It's a bit of a hog-tussle down here."

A column of pine trees explode into flames near Flynn's left flank. The plane is at risk of being both sucked into the raging wildfire and flipped by the fireballs erupting from beneath it. As sparking embers *tink* off the windscreen, the plane dives. With fierce concentration, Flynn wrestles the controls, and the sounds around him blend into white noise. Over the din, he hears the faint sound of Chuck's voice on the radio. "Drop it... You're there, buddy!"

Flynn's hand reaches over to actuate the release of the water tanks. The handling of the airplane eases as the load is dropped, and Flynn breathes a heavy sigh from the exertion. Like a mystical dragon being repelled, the wildfire responds to the water drop with an angry hiss. The Catalina's engines throttle up again, and the aircraft slowly rises toward the spotter plane circling above. Flynn slowly climbs out of the smoky haze, pulling back steadily on the yoke. The radio crackles to life again as Chuck comments, "Great drop, Flynn! You really laid it low and put it where it counts!"

The Catalina continues to climb away from the flaming timber below and banks toward the lake. The gleeful chirp in Chuck's voice over the radio is near celebratory. "Let's go do some splash 'n drops like the Old Man said!"

Flynn wipes beads of sweat from his face and steers the aircraft toward the heavens. He tilts the wing in a steep turning bank and swoops in alongside Chuck in the spotter plane. "Copy that, pard! It will be good to get a little wet, and cool off my belly some… " Looking out his side window, Flynn clearly sees Chuck in the other airplane cockpit and gives him a thumbs-up.

As they fly side by side over the fire-damaged terrain, the mountain lake can be seen in the far distance. Flynn looks out over the landscape and inherently knows that this is his time and place. Chuck's voice comes back over the radio. "Hey, Buddy! I just got a call from base." The radio cuts out, and returns. "It seems that Madam Ball-buster is packing her bags and heading on to another gig somewhere else."

Flynn stares ahead, taking in the view from his office of the day. He looks to the multiple columns of smoke rising up and feels a calm, sense of peace. Memories of his relationship with Camille briefly flit through his mind, before he returns to the present moment. He brings his microphone closer to his mouth and replies, "Yeah, I heard something about that…"

Chuck continues, "If we complete the contracts we just picked up, we might make it for another season…"

Flynn seems mesmerized by lingering thoughts of lost love and an airborne perspective of the expanse below. "That's good news, Chuck…" He wipes away a bit of sweat that drips, like a tear, from the corner of his eye and states, "Another good day of flying is all we can hope for."

~*~

As the airplanes roar over the lake, Flynn scans the water's surface before diving lower. Banking at the far end, the Catalina seaplane comes around and then dips low to skim through the rolling waves. The radio sizzles with static, as Flynn concentrates on using the water scoopers to fill the drop tanks. With a somber tone, Chuck's voice comes on the line again. "Hey Flynn… The Old Man just dropped me a message to let me know about Woody."

Fire Angels

The Catalina skims across the surface of the lake, toward the submerged wreck of the C-130 tanker. Flynn holds steady on the controls, noticing the crashed airplane pass under his starboard wingtip, and then looks ahead as he quickly approaches a wall of flaming trees on the shoreline. He glances to the water level gauge on the drop tanks and then assesses the distance needed to safely lift off.

Through the background noise, the voice on the radio interrupts Flynn's concentration. "Hey pal... Ol' Woody has got his wings back... I bet he's up there having a drink with Chip right now."

As the water tanks top off, Flynn closes the scoops and eases the yoke back all the way to his chest. The heavy water-bird slowly lifts off the lake's surface and thunders skyward. Flynn releases a sigh and glances up to the spotter plane circling high above. "Yeah, you're probably right..."

The vintage flying boat lifts off the lake's surface, leaving a trailing wake on the shimmering, fire-tinted water. The v-shaped ripple of waves rolls across the water, passing over the submerged wreckage of the C-130 tanker. In the sky, the distinctive silhouettes of two fire-bombing aircrafts roar over the flaming treetops along the lakeshore before heading toward the distant mountains on the smoky horizon.

The End.

If you enjoyed **Fire Angels**, read other stories by
Eric H. Heisner
www.leandogproductions.com

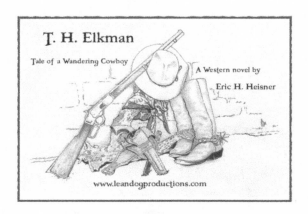

Eric H. Heisner is an award-winning writer, actor and filmmaker. He is the author of several Western and Adventure novels: *West to Bravo, T. H. Elkman, Africa Tusk, Conch Republic* and *Short Western Tales: Friend of the Devil*. He can be contacted at his website:

www.leandogproductions.com

Adeline Emmalei is a creative artist, student and animal lover. She lives in Austin, Texas.